The Fresh French Connection

The Fresh French Connection

Annie Mick

Copyright

Table of Contents

Prologue

When you're young and unafraid, the world is yours to conquer. The plan is to take it by storm – be it a hurricane, tornado or tsunami. You're unstoppable.

Yet it seems every woman I come across – literally or figuratively speaking – is waiting for me to place the rock on her finger and say those magic words "I do"; to promise her the world.

Ah, yes. Have I told you I literally have an allergy to those two words? Seriously, they cause my skin to itch. An ugly rash breaks out and I run like my ass is on fire for the nearest door so fast it's more akin to a dance that not only causes it to rain, but avalanches roar down the mountains in other countries, earthquakes shake the ground so fiercely the Richter scale proves useless, the ocean floor rumbles so violently vibrations can be felt from one coast to the other, and bears leave hibernation to escape the echoes reaching the depths of where they've burrowed.

Matrimony. The very word leaves a taste on my tongue so acrid I tend to bite it hard enough to draw blood and leave a metallic taste to masque it.

Marriage leads to children; those little urchins that burp and regurgitate, leaving stains on your shirt that are impossible to remove. Have you ever seen a baby projectile vomit? You can use them as a weapon in the grocery store. I suppose they could come in handy for Black Friday shopping. "Stay back or my kid will shoot! That 56-inch screen TV is mine!"

And diapers. Need I say more? In case I do, they don't always hold what's been deposited into them. Those safety deposit wrappers hold no guarantee. You will never see FDIC advertising on those packages.

No, I swore off marriage and kids when I was in the seventh grade as I watched a woman changing a baby at a football game on the grass at the side of the bleachers. They should have brought her a fire hose – for all the good it would have done. The poor kid shot shit from his head to his toes in a onesie outfit.

And I thought oranges were hard to peel.

But my mother has always had her heart set on grandchildren.

Someone really should have told her to have more than one offspring.

Chapter 1

"Do you ever date them more than once?"

Colton's question is nothing unusual; simply intriguing. He's my best friend; has been since we were kids. We were little league champs, boarding school roomies, and now college pre-law students as well as football champion man whores – sort of. We're both football champions, I'm the champion man whore. The real difference between us? Colton has a conscience. I fall somewhere between caring about the general wellbeing of my friends and getting the hell out the door before my latest conquest wakes up. I don't fix the women breakfast, I don't do walks in the park, and handholding serves one purpose – holding them down while you drill them from above.

We share a condo off the campus of Boston University that Colton's grandfather – the formidable Briggs Kinkaid – purchased to keep us out of the frat houses, aka out of trouble. It's out of the way of student traffic, off limits to overnight boner seekers and succubi, and provides the peaceful sanctuary that we both need to acquire and maintain the 4.0 GPA requisite to continue our lifestyle.

"Colt, you know me. I'm a slip in and slip out kind of guy. I don't date," I reply and pretend to shudder. "Date rhymes with mate and that is the last thing I'm looking for. The two phrases I never want to hear in this lifetime are 'I do' and 'I'm late'." I give him a stern warning, emphasizing while counting off on my fingers, "Three worst words in the English language; date, mate and late."

"Speaking of which," he says, rolling his eyes and grabbing his duffle in the foyer. "Practice starts in half an hour. Coach is going to make us do sprints for half of practice if we're late. Let's go."

"I'm coming, let me grab my bag." As we walk out the door, Grayson Kibbey pulls up to the curb. Grayson is the other star of the team, the second major dick on campus – I've had the lead role since freshman year – two positions we take quite seriously. Grayson's a bit of a double dipper and loves to brag about it. I like my triples, but I'm not a conversationalist. If the ladies discuss it, that's on them, but I've found informing them they'll never get a second ride on the Chambers rocket – should they broadcast our activities – it has a strong tendency to keep them discreet. I believe discretion is the better part of valor. That, and the coach would be showing us films and lecturing about double wrapping again… and again. The women never get a second ride regardless, but it keeps them hopeful and generally quiet . . . after we're done in the bedroom.

"Colt and I were having an interesting discussion inside," I tell Grayson as I squeeze inside the backseat of his BMW. "He wants to know why I don't date the women I fuck."

Grayson slaps the steering wheel and laughs loudly, pulling out onto the quiet street. "Damn, that's a good one Colt. Conversation *and* sex." He scrunches his brow as if considering the thought himself and shakes his head. "Nope, can't picture it. Although I do whisper some pretty filthy things in their ears. Does conversation *with* sex count?"

Colton reaches over and punches his arm. "Just drive, asshole." He puffs out a sigh. "Have either of you ever even taken a woman out to dinner?"

"I took my mom out for Italian just last month for her birthday," Kibbey answers defensively with a short nod as if he should be commended.

"I believe gentleman Kinkaid is under the impression we should woo them," I elucidate from the back seat.

"Woo them?" Grayson laughs. "Sorry, Colt, I'd rather screw them. Get in, get out."

"You must be short on foreplay, Kibbey." Colton smirks, glancing over his seat back at me.

"What the hell are you talking about?" Kibbey shoots him a glare.

Colton shrugs and tosses Gray a shit eating grin. "You *get* in and get out. Chambers here…" He points to me over his shoulder, "…*slips* in and slips out. Sounds to me like he gives them more of a warmup."

Kibbey grumbles incoherently as we pull into the stadium parking lot; something about assholes, do just fine, my tongue, wet pussies, and they love my dick. Or was that lick? Doesn't matter, I'm the lead man whore.

Chapter 2

Girlfriend is a dirty word

So, Colton's got himself a girlfriend. The inevitable cliff you fall off when you find someone to take the leap with you. I'm not a heights person myself so I'll never know how that feels. I fly all the time, I've even bungee jumped. But counting on someone else to catch me if I fall? Hard pass. Taking the plunge? I do, regularly. The fact that it's into a different woman a couple times a week is convenient. It keeps my dick warm, my heart cold, and my conscience clear.

I saw Jana first. I tried to pick her up at the bar that night, but the woman wouldn't even look at me twice. She was too busy nursing a glass of water and guarding the drinks on the table so no one could slip a mickey in them. She is a beautiful woman, and I may have gone more than one round with her; who knows? Hell, I may have even fixed her breakfast.

It was the night after the game in which Colt got hit square in the balls by a helmet. Poor bastard didn't see it coming and none of us could head it off. He still showed up to the bar though. I've often wondered what would have happened if he hadn't? What if he had gone home and iced his balls like he should have? Would

Jana have given in and danced with me? Would I have eventually talked her into going back to her place? I'm happy for him . . . I really am. But it's confusing when I don't know if I'm jealous of him for having something reliable or jealous of her for taking a piece of my best friend away as well as his time. I'm a little mad at him for giving a piece away as well as his time. I'm mad at her for having that piece and not being willing to give hers to me when I saw her first. I don't really think it's Jana per se; it's the situation. *I don't trust it.*

It's also Colton's home situation. It sucks. His folks are . . . the Kinkaids. They are the money of Essex Junction, Vermont. I used to think my mom was pushy. If anyone has ever made me appreciate my mom more, it's Mrs. Kinkaid. It wasn't intentional on her part, believe me. All she had to do was exist. The woman makes Joan Crawford look like a saint. Colton's an only kid too; has never had a steady girlfriend, and latched onto Jana like the world revolves around her. I don't know, maybe it does . . .

One thing I do know . . . I would never wait a year for a woman. But I guess he has. Where the hell did the Colton Kinkaid I know go? He waited a year to get into her panties. A year?! That's 365 opportunities he's passed up. Scratch that – 366. It's leap year.

Junior year and I'm still as tainted as I always was, always will be, and have no plans to change.

Graduation Boston U

Hello, Europe! Here we come. Our plans haven't changed, and Jana has encouraged Colton to stick with them to the end. If he had backed out on this trip, I'm not sure I could have ever forgiven him. Freshman year, we planned this trek across Europe. It's our celebratory trip in honor of making it through the first four years of college. The next three are going to be a bitch and we'll be at opposite ends of the country. Now is the time.

Graduation is upon us and one week from now we will be on a plane to start a one-month journey backpacking through Europe. Truth be told, we'll probably end up eating the finest of foods in France, staying in luxe hotels, sitting on our asses, drinking to our hearts' content, walking the streets until our feet get tired and going back for more liquor.

After it's over, Colton and I will be separated for the first time in our lives; for three years while I go to Stanford University and he stays here in Boston. We were supposed to do Stanford together, but now my plan is to return to open our practice in Vermont. We'll see what happens. I've found in the last three years that things can change drastically. Even Kibbey changed his mind and decided to stay on the east coast. Colt and I haven't lost our connection; we have an additive in the form of Jana Cooper. It was unrealistic to think things would remain the same in adulthood. I just never expected our lives to change so much in such a short amount of time.

The original plan, per our parents, was for us to go to

Harvard. It was an easy in – our fathers are alumni – but we had our own plans, our own scenario, and the determination to make it work. We're now four years into it, three to go, and Grayson is on board as well. Corporate attorneys in a cushy life, three partners with our own secretaries, regular hours, home on time every night, being our own bosses. All of us have trust funds we could live on for three lifetimes. If we had no ambition, I suppose we could live as beach bums, spending our days watching bikini clad bodies walk by, collecting them one-by-one, sending them home when we're through. The very thought of it gives me a headache and makes me nauseous. I don't mind relaxing, taking a vacation here and there, getting laid on a regular basis, but idle hands and an idle brain would send me to an early grave.

Europe

"If I hear you whine one more time about how much you miss her," I warn Colton, "I will put my foot so far up your ass, my toes will be kicking your teeth out."

This is our second week here and we're backpacking through rough terrain – have been for two days – and the poor pussy hasn't been able to reach his girlfriend. If he lifts his cell phone up toward heaven one more time to check for reception, I will send him there personally. Maybe God can give him a direct line to talk to Jana. Can you imagine the intro to that conversation?

"Hello, Jana. This is God speaking. I have your boyfriend here due to an unfortunate incident between him and his former friend, Sebastian. I'll let you talk to him one last time because once he's here, well, he's here to stay. That, and I'm so tired of hearing him whine. No, no, my dear, there are no reversals. Once you're dead, you're dead. I'll keep him safe until your demise. You'll see him then. Make this conversation count, it's the last one you'll get for a while. Oh, and don't hesitate to count on Sebastian for comfort."

Where the hell did that last thought come from?

"I just want to check in with her, make sure everything's alright," he says. "I told her I would stay in touch."

"Why the hell are we here, Colt?" I yell, throwing my hands in the air. "You've been attached at the hip for the last three fucking years! You can't take one month to breathe? For God's sake, you should have left your balls with her! She already owns them."

He scowls. "Not funny, Chambers. You know, if you'd stop treating pussy like an ice cream store that adds a new flavor every week needing to be sampled, you might find one you like."

I stare at him for a moment before the laughter rumbles from my chest. "That's a good one, Kinkaid. Me, one woman for the rest of my life, white picket fence." I shake my head and pierce him a glare. "Not gonna happen . . . ever."

He rolls his eyes and slaps my shoulder. "I'll put the damn phone away. You're right. This vacation is ours and Jannie will be there when I get back."

"Atta boy," I say as I pat him on the back. "I'm gonna miss you next year, Colt. Let's make the best of what we've got here. We'll finish out this hike and we'll hit the hotels and drink ourselves into a stupor . . . for days on end."

He sighs heavily and shakes his head. "We're not backpacking anymore for the rest of the trip, are we?"

"Why bother?" I bob my eyebrows. "I've heard the gelato here is delicious."

He drops his chin to his chest with a groan. "Great. Just don't bring Ms. Gelato back to our room."

We start walking again, backpacks strapped to our shoulders. I look to him, smirking. "Where did you come up with your lame ice cream example? You know my idea of dessert is a second cheeseburger and another beer."

* * *

We're sitting on the patio of a street café in the middle of Paris enjoying a morning latte and croissants – my stomach roiling a bit from too much alcohol, my head pounding from an insufferable hangover.

I am officially pussified. Latte? Croissants? Whatever happened to black coffee and pancakes? Maybe bacon and waffles? Somebody find me a double espresso and an order of sausage and scrambled eggs . . . fast. The waiter continues to fill my water glass as I drain it each time to replenish my dehydrated body.

The sunglasses on my face help shade my eyes from simple daylight as the sun is nonexistent today. The sky is mostly overcast, a dim gray color that matches the wet sidewalks after a light rain this morning.

"Feeling human yet?" Colt asks.

"Ask me again at –" I glance at my watch seeing a time of only ten, "– noon." My voice is gravelly and harsh. I'm sure my liver has seen better days as well.

"When do your parents get in?"

Shit. I thought my head was going to explode before. I'm supposed to drop Colt off to catch his flight back home today, and in two days I pick my folks up to spend the next two weeks with them . . . here. Can you say joy? Yeah, neither can I.

I love my folks. They're good people; classy, kind, charitable, loving. But the thought of spending two weeks in Europe with them after I've already been here for a month is excruciatingly painful. That eye roll I just finished as the thoughts ran through my head? Very painful.

"Day after tomorrow," I reply. "Sure you don't want to stay?" I lower my shades below the bridge of my nose so he can see the pleading in my eyes.

He smiles. The asshole actually smiles…slyly no less. "That would be a hard, harsh, absolutely not. I'm going home to my ball owner."

I drop my upper half onto the tabletop, dramatically expressing my disappointment with a groan. "Colt, please. Don't make me do this alone."

I feel a soft touch on my back as it gently glides its way to my shoulder.

"Est-ce que ca va? Puis-je vous aider?" It's the voice of an angel wanting to know if I'm okay and if she can help me.

I don't have to look up to see her to know how beautiful she is – it's in her voice. Worse yet? The sound doesn't shoot straight to my dick. It's hitting somewhere between my shoulders and my belly and makes me slightly fuzzy.

I lift my head slowly and find myself speechless at the vision before me. What the hell is going on? The only thing between my shoulders and belly is kidneys, liver, spleen, gallbladder… And what's that caught in my throat? I try to swallow but my mouth is dry.

She has beautiful brown eyes flecked with gold, long dark hair. She's tall, thin, has small breasts – nothing magazine worthy – but her smile takes my breath away. Her hand is still on my shoulder and the heat it transfers onto my skin makes me want to lean into her, wrap my arms around her waist and hold her close to me.

"Est-ce que ca va?" she asks again. She places the hand she had on my shoulder to her chest. *"Tu m'as inqui'et'e."* I worried her.

Colton laughs loudly and waves his hand, dismissing my actions. "Il va bien. Il est dramatique." *Thanks asshole. Yeah, I'll be fine, and I wasn't being dramatic!*

She giggles and I hear angels sing. *What the hell is wrong with me?*

Colton looks at his watch and rises from his chair. "I'm going to grab my things from the room. I'll meet you back here. Finish your coffee." He walks away before I can respond. Not that I could; I'm too enamored by the vision before me.

"Puis-je vous offrir quelque chose d'autre?" she asks. Aw, she wants to know if she can get me anything. Her eyes still have me stunned. Her voice is sultry, sweet.

"I-I'm…"

"I speak English," she says with a thick accent. "Would that help? Which do you prefer?"

I take a deep breath and let it out. "I think…I prefer you. What's your name?"

She laughs softly. "I am Nina. We just did a shift change. I'll be your server. I can bring you fresh coffee."

"Can you watch a sunset with me tonight, Nina?"

Her eyes open wide, and her mouth forms a perfect O. Surprisingly, her reaction still doesn't shoot straight to my dick. She tucks her hair behind her ear and smiles shyly. "I'd like that. I am done here at six o'clock."

I reach for her hand, take it in mine and place a kiss on her knuckles. "I'll be back at six, Nina. I'm Sebastian. I look forward to it."

* * *

"I'll see you when you get back," Colton says before he closes the car door. "Have fun with the 'rents."

"You're a funny man, Kinkaid." I scowl.

He dips his head down one last time and shoots me a pointed look. "Hey, better yours than mine. Tell mama Chambers hello and give her a hug for me."

"You got it," I tell him. "Give Jana a hug and remind her I'm always up for…" The door slams. I smile to myself as I take off in the rental car. I'm always teasing Colt about having a threesome. He knows it's a joke. What are friends for?

* * *

I'm back at the café at five minutes before six. I tucked a blanket from the hotel into the car to spread out underneath us to watch the sunset. I have a basket packed with grapes, cheese, bread and a bottle of wine. The perfect complement to a perfect evening.

Don't ask me what I'm doing. I have not one fucking clue. Remember? I don't fix them breakfast. I'm out the door before they wake up. Why would a snack seem such a contrast to breakfast? Probably because Nina is such a contrast to the women I'm used to using…uh, seeing.

She runs to the car when she spots me sitting outside. I had every intention of going inside to escort her to the car, but I hadn't had a chance to get out before she was bounding out the door and hopping inside.

We go to a beach in Marseilles. It's crowded – far too crowded for my liking. Nina has me turn the car around and directs me to a quiet, out of the way place near the banks of the Seine with a grassy area where we spread the blanket and take our seats in the middle. I unload the basket and place the containers around us to pick and choose from as we please.

I've never had a woman feed me grapes before, but she does it with such ease and finesse; her fingertips teasing the edges of my mouth as my lips close over the crisp fruit. The look in her eyes as she watches my mouth while she feeds me is tempting, yet playful and innocent.

We spend hours lying on the blanket, watching the sunset, waiting for the stars to come out after. We talk about my life in the States, her life in France, our goals, family, friends. We kiss, cuddle, explore each other's bodies in gentle, rather unhurried ways. It's easy and comfortable. She's unlike any woman I've ever met. I want to take my time, memorize every inch of her before I have to leave.

"Nina," I murmur against her mouth as my hands reach higher and higher under her blouse; her back arching under my touch, her moans urging me on. "We should take this back to my hotel room."

"No," she whispers, fisting my shirt. "Right here is fine. I want you to take me here. We don't have time to go back to your room. I must be home by midnight. Mon maman et papa will be waiting for me."

My hands freeze on her rib cage and slowly slide out from under her blouse. I can suddenly feel the one organ I didn't mention between my shoulders and rib cage . . . my heart. I know that sonofabitch exists now because it just took off from the starting line at the Indy 500 and is announcing its presence, at approximately 160 beats per minute.

"Nina," I mutter. "How old are you?"

She continues to work at the buttons on my shirt. "Old enough, Bast. I am older than my years, older in my mind than in my body."

"Nina," I prompt with warning as I grip her shoulders gently and lean my forehead on hers. "Don't lie to me. How old are you?"

"Sixteen," she says. "But I . . ."

"Sixteen," I repeat, my head swimming somewhere between

disbelief and fury, and the heart I've always sworn I didn't have sinks to my belly.

Jailbait. Jailbait.

I rise to my feet like my ass is on fire. I throw the items laid out on the blanket into the basket, take her hand and pull her to her feet, gathering the blanket and wadding it into a ball under my arm. I don't know what the statutory rape laws are in France, but I have no intention of being on the receiving end of charges for it.

I turn and walk towards the car, tossing a grunt over my shoulder, "Let's go."

"S`ebastien!" she shouts a desperate plea as she stumbles behind me. It pierces my heart a little as I love the way she says my name, but it also now leaves a pit in my stomach with the knowledge that she is so far out of reach.

Sixteen! Legal in dog years, maybe. Jail time in real life. I would have sworn she was at least nineteen.

We ride in silence for the first few minutes. My grip on the steering wheel turns my knuckles white and Nina stares out the window on her side of the car. I hear her sniffle a couple of times and glance over when her hand rises to swipe a tear away.

I'm seven years older than she is, I remind myself. Ten years from now it might not matter. Hell, even five years, but today . . . so fucking innocent.

Taking a deep breath before snapping the way I feel I should, I simply say, "Give me an address. I'll drop you off."

She reluctantly gives me directions and I pull up to her building located in the 17th arrondissement. There is foot traffic on the sidewalks, cars passing by. I'm not sure this is beneficial or not; I could be identified.

"I'll wait for you, Bast," she whispers. "When you come back, I'll be here."

"Nina," I protest, slowly shaking my head. I refuse to look at her – it'll hurt. I know it will. And I don't hurt over women, ever. Moreover, and more importantly, I don't want to hurt her. I approached her at the café today. I have never felt guilt over a woman; I pleasure them, they pleasure me. Done. But Nina . . .

How she affected me the way she did, I will never know.

"Look at me, S`ebastien." She grips my chin firmly in her small hand and turns my head so I can't look away. "You know where to find me. I won't always be this young."

I gaze into eyes that are rimmed with tears, pain so obvious and deep it breaks my heart – that organ I refuse to acknowledge.

"Nina," I whisper, squeezing my eyes closed. Before I can stop her, her lips are touching mine, taking one last kiss. I relish her softness, the way her mouth fits against mine, the way she tastes, the forbidden pleasure. When the kiss is over, I feel empty, bereft, like a part of me has been stripped away.

"You will miss me, S`ebastien Chambers," she says confidently. "There are too many sunsets to see, too many stars to watch come out at night." She palms my cheek, running her fingers gently through my scruff; the sensation so overwhelming it's suffocating. "Count them with me even when we're apart. Come back to me and we will count them together."

I reach for her this time, desperately needing one last taste, and kiss her softly. "Don't wait for me, Nina. You can do so much better."

I watch as she walks to the building and slips inside. That organ that I have refused to acknowledge for so many years? Yeah, it hurts like a sonofabitch.

* * *

Two weeks later, after spending an infinite amount of time with my parents traveling from place to place – sightseeing, shopping, visiting museums – we're back in Paris for one last day before heading home.

"Hey guys, I need to run out for a bit to grab something. I'll be right back," I tell them, my hand on the knob, ready to walk out the door.

"Where are you headed, Sebastian?" mom asks. "Maybe I can go with you."

"That's okay, I'll only be a couple minutes." I close the door behind me before she can protest. One more glance, it's all I need for closure.

I make my way down the sidewalk across the street from the tiny café where Colton and I spent the last morning he was here. I see her waiting the tables of the latte and espresso drinkers; pouring their drinks, dropping off croissants and pastries. She's busy, but she moves like a ballerina between the tables. Her smile falters from time to time, but she's confident, strong, graceful. She's – dare I say – poetry in motion.

One last look. One last dose of Nina before I fly back across an ocean away from her. I know it's crazy. She's just a girl – a young girl. She looks up, her brow furrowed as she glances around, searching. Is the pull so strong between us that she can feel me watching her? I've gotta get out of here, but before I can turn away, she spots me, and our eyes meet. She places an inward clenched fist to her chest, smiles softly, and releases her hand to wave goodbye.

Damned hearts.

Chapter 3

Don't say I didn't tell you

"What do you mean she left?" I yell at Mrs. Kinkaid. Dumb bitch could have gotten a hold of me. One phone call is all it would have taken. "Why the fuck didn't you call me?"

She gasps and places a hand to her chest as if insulted and taken aback at my swearing. *Oh please.*

Colton's lying in a hospital bed in a coma after being hit by a drunk driver half an hour away from home. He never made it back from Europe. Grayson knew nothing about it until I called him. Mrs. Kinkaid hadn't called anyone until I got home. Scratch that. The bitch hadn't called anyone…except for Jana. My mother's friends at the country club found out and called my mother. And Jana hadn't called me, which makes zero sense at all. Until…

"Jana came after I called her, Sebastian," Mrs. Kinkaid says. "But she didn't even stay for an hour. Can you believe that? My Colton was in surgery! She left me sitting there by myself! She couldn't find the time to stay long enough to see if he made it through." She cries against my shoulder, leaning heavily in my arms. "She came back the second day, waiting for the doctor's report. As soon as she heard spinal injury, she couldn't get out of here fast enough. She had the nerve to say she couldn't handle a cripple!" she screams. "Can you imagine how I felt? How could she walk away and leave the burden of it all to me?"

Yes, Mrs. Kinkaid, let's make this all about you.

"Why didn't you call Grayson . . . or me?"

"I was too upset to call anyone else. What that Jana did was just too much." She cries more, sobbing into my shoulder. I've never been a fan of Mrs. Kinkaid, but she is his mother. Maybe this will make her a better human being, a better mother, make her appreciate the man Colton is. Better late than never, I suppose. I'll give her the benefit of the doubt.

I walk her to the nearest chair to help her get seated. "Tell me the rest," I say, patting her shoulder, handing her more tissues.

"What else is there to say?" She sniffs indignantly. "I told Colton a long time ago she was trash. I knew she was only after his money."

"Just try, okay?" I prod.

My blood boils as I listen to the horror story the woman tells. My best friend – so lost in love that he couldn't see straight – abandoned in his time of need. He bought her engagement ring in Europe!

The formidable Briggs Kinkaid makes his appearance known as he enters the hallway and walks towards us, his heavy footsteps announcing his arrival.

"Sebastian," he acknowledges me with a sharp nod. His eyes are worn with worry, the bags underneath them show signs of lost sleep for days on end. "Karlene," he addresses his daughter-in-law, "Why don't you go home, I'll stay with Colton."

"I don't know if I want…" she begins to protest.

"Go home, Karlene." He shoots her a glare that leaves no room for argument. "Sebastian and I will stay with him."

The power this man holds is evident when Mrs. Kinkaid stands and walks away without another word. The truth is Briggs Kinkaid takes no shit…from anyone. And he holds a strong disdain for his daughter-in-law and has never failed to hide it. Briggs loves Colton; pretty much worships the ground he walks on. Something parents should do when a kid is young, but Colton's never have; and Briggs has held it against them since the day Colton was born.

Briggs and I enter the room where Colton lies in a bed, tubes entering or exiting practically every orifice possible, machines beeping as they monitor various body functions. He looks like shit; bruises in different stages of healing, one leg casted and held in a traction unit, an arm casted all the way to his shoulder, head still bandaged in wraps covering staples that were placed for gashes. All on the left side.

"Jesus," I mutter as I study his nearly lifeless body.

"No," Briggs snaps. "This is Colton. You call out *that* name, you'd better be praying. He can use every damn one of them."

"I'm going to cancel Stanford," I tell him. "I'll get set up with Boston."

He snaps his head up, his brow furrowed. "Why?"

I look to where Colton lies in the bed and slowly lift my head and meet Briggs' eyes, determination set in my own.

"Because when he wakes up, we're going to get his ass out of this bed and he's going to walk, and he's going to finish school, and we're going to open that practice, just like we planned."

Briggs nods once. "You're going to make a great team, son."

The Wake-up Call

Three weeks after the accident Colton woke up from that damn coma. I'm not a crier, never have been, but I cried that day. Then I cried harder when he recognized me and squeezed my hand with his right one. Grayson and I pretty much camped out at that hospital day and night, reading to him, watching movies on TV and teasing him about missing the porn, begging him to open his eyes. Jana's name was never mentioned.

He glanced around the room at the faces that were present, studied mine for a time questioning where she was, and when I lowered my eyes and grimaced, he closed his. I watched as a single tear fell and rolled to his ear. We haven't spoken her name since. I imagine someday we might, probably not.

* * *

"You can do this, Colt," I encourage as he struggles along the bars on each side of him, taking slow awkward steps one at a time as the male therapist holds the gait belt strapped around his mid-section. He's fighting hard, it hurts. The anger in his eyes, the redness in his cheeks, the set jaw as he drags another foot forward is painful to watch. But if I give up on my best friend, who's to say he won't give up on himself? Grayson and I are his cheering section. We're not going to fail him.

He goes home in six days to therapy coming in twice a day to work with him there. Unfortunately, home to Colton means his parents' house. It's the only option. The summer is over and school is about to start. Grayson and I need to get our asses back to Boston and start law school. Colt will be a year behind us, but that law office will have his name on a plaque waiting for him to join us.

And Jana? Who the hell knows? Should I see her in Boston – as was her plan for continuing her education – I will make it my life's mission to make hers a living hell. She won't last long at Boston – I'll see to that personally.

The Real Wake-up Call

My first weekend back from Boston – the first weekend after school started – I stop to check on Colt. School isn't far from home, so I plan on coming back every weekend, at least until he's on his feet and moving around on his own without the need of a wheelchair on a regular basis.

"He's in his room," Mrs. Kinkaid tells me. "He'll be happy to see you, Sebastian. His mood hasn't been too good lately. I just don't know what to do with him."

It's not what you do with him; it's what you do for him, you dumb bitch!

I open the door to his room, knowing he can't get to it easily to open it for me.

"Hey, Colt," I announce myself before stepping in. I get no response, so I step in farther. "Oh fuck, what did you do?" I scream. His head is flopped back in the wheelchair, his body limp; a bottle of tequila lies spilled on the floor next to it, and an empty pill bottle is on the floor next to that.

"Call 9-1-1!" I yell out the door. I rush to where he sits in the wheelchair, lean him forward and he groans with the movement. *Good, you stupid ass! You're still alive!* I stick my fingers down his throat until he gags and pukes. Some of the pills haven't dissolved and are coming up in chunks.

"What's going on?" Mrs. Kinkaid asks as she reaches the door.

"Call 9-1-1!" I scream at her…again.

She gasps. "Colton, what have you…"

"Call!" I scream for the third time.

I pull him up out of the chair, bend him over and make him puke again. Better crippled than dead, Colt. Although I am going to kick your ass when this is over.

The ambulance arrives, the paramedics take over. I hand over the empty pill bottle – painkillers no less – and let them do their thing. Now we wait and see.

"He did what?" Grayson's tone is flat as he takes in the news I've delivered via phone. He's scared, shocked, waiting for the other shoe to drop. "Is he…is he…?"

"They've pumped his stomach, flushed his system," I tell him. "He's out of it right now. We're waiting. It's all we can do."

"I'll be there in a couple hours," he says.

"Gray, there's nothing you can do."

I hear a car door slam in the background as he growls into the phone. "I said I'll be there in a couple hours."

* * *

"Neuro testing looks good," the doctor says, holding the chart and flipping through the sheets as he studies each one. "No long-term effects from the overdose. It's a good thing you got to him when you did. Much later and he wouldn't…"

"When can you release him?" I ask before letting him finish the statement we all don't need to hear. Grayson and I stand together, a united front. We've already decided what needs to be done. Now it's all in the timing for getting it done. If Colt goes back to his parents' house, he'll do it again. If he goes to a facility, he'll feel abandoned. There's no way in hell we'll let that happen. If it were one of us, he'd be the first in line to do whatever it took to get us through.

"We need to hold him for 72 hours. It's mandatory for suicide attempts," the doctor informs us.

"You've had him for two days," I state. "So, you release him tomorrow. Correct?"

He sighs heavily. "His parents want…"

"I don't give a rat's ass what his parents want," I yell. "He's an adult and it was his parents that let this happen in the first place!"

We hear footsteps clomping in the hall, making their way towards us. Their heavy, rushed, and sound an awful lot like Briggs Kinkaid.

"His parents have no jurisdiction over the boy, Milton." Yup, it was Briggs' footsteps. Hear them once, you'll never forget them. The man's name should be plastered over every hospital wing in Vermont – big donator, board of directors, etc. "I have durable power of attorney. I will make the decisions. Who the hell have you been talking to?"

The doctor stutters, his cheeks flushing, "M-Mrs. Kinkaid told me…"

"Karlene's a thorn in my ass," Briggs roars. "Get Colton ready to go. Now."

"But regulations state…"

Briggs glares and gives his order one more time through a clenched jaw, "Now."

"Yes, sir. But you understand if I release him it's against…"

Briggs brushes him off with a wave of his hand. "I'll deal with the board."

The doctor turns and walks down the hallway towards the nurses' station. I watch as he stops, handing paperwork to the nurse as he speaks with her while she bobs her head up and down, shooting glances in our direction.

Briggs folds his arms over his chest and eyes us skeptically. "What are you boys up to?"

"I want to take Colt back to Boston with me," I reply. Briggs may be formidable, but I'm not too shabby myself when challenged.

His eyes widen as his brows shoot skyward. "You what? What about the girl?"

Shaking my head, a low growl leaving my throat, I inform him, "She's not there. I already checked. Jana's long gone. Grayson and I have a first-floor apartment. We'll make it work. We'll get him 24-hour care, get him to therapy appointments." My stomach churns when I recall seeing him in that wheelchair two days ago. "But the one thing he will not have is access to painkillers. He can do this with ibuprofen or Tylenol. Maybe some muscle cream."

He thinks on it for a few moments, his eyes flitting between Grayson and myself. "How many bedrooms in your apartment?"

Grayson screws his eyebrows and his mouth twists. "Two?"

Briggs shoots him a scolding glare as if he's schooling him in the fine art of business; that, and the teacher is losing patience. "Mine was the question, boy. You were supposed to answer."

It's almost humorous watching Grayson squirm under Briggs' scrutiny. "Uh, two, sir. It has two."

Briggs nods firmly. "We'll make it three. I'll get it done today. Colton will stay with me for the next few days while you two get set up. You've missed enough school as it is. I'll send you the new address and get the movers scheduled. Come back Saturday and we'll make the trip together to get you settled in."

He starts down the hall towards Colt's room, then stops and walks back to where we stand. He raises a finger, stern warning in his voice and his steely grey eyes that leaves no room for compromise. "There will be no parties, no liquor, and no wild women in and out at all hours. Do I make myself clear?"

In unison, Gray and I voice compliance, "Yes, sir."

He spins on his heel to take his leave. He hesitates at about his tenth step and we hear him heave a deep sigh and watch him shake his head. "At least not until he's fully recovered."

And just like that we all became roomies.

* * *

"I don't need a damn babysitter," Colt growls, throwing a dish in the sink with his left hand while bracing himself with a crutch under his right arm.

We've been sharing a three-bedroom apartment with Grayson for two months now. A damn nice apartment, I might add. Colton still has therapy two times a day for strengthening exercises as well as resistance training, and specialized therapists to help him regain muscle control. We also have a housekeeper, a cook, laundry service, and every other amenity a person could imagine, all complements of Briggs Kinkaid. I'm used to luxury – we all are – but over the past four years we had gotten used to doing things for ourselves and didn't mind it. Having the option of being lazy is one thing, having it shoved down your throat is another.

Colt's having a severe problem with surveillance for anywhere from twelve to sixteen hours a day while Grayson and I are gone, and not having the place to himself. It's not as if the help hangs on him, never leaving his side – they're just here in the same apartment. But at night, it's just the three of us – no booze, no broads, and no company – per Colton's preference.

"You don't need someone giving you a bath anymore." I shrug. "Baby steps, Colt." Feigning a dreamy sigh I add, "If it had been me though, I would have played it up and hung onto that big-titted redhead for a while longer. Did you ever play with those while she was washing your…"

"Fuck off, Chambers." The daggers he shoots me from angry eyes doesn't stop me. He needs that anger. It's a driving force to keep him working hard to recuperate.

"No, seriously," I continue to provoke him. "I would have pretended to be adjusting myself and grabbed a quick nip right through that uniform." I flash him a smile. "She would have had that top off in two seconds flat."

"Are you quite finished?" he grinds through a clenched jaw.

"Nope," I say with a grin. "I'm thinking you could have sat up quickly, grabbed her around the waist, stripped her out of those pants and she would have ridden you hard in no time." I shrug again. "It's not like you weren't already naked."

"You don't give up, do you?"

"No, I don't," I say flatly, matching his scathing glare. "And neither do you. And I'll be damned if I let you start now. Two months, Colt. You'll be running beside Gray and me. We'll hit the gym every fucking day. I promise. Whatever it takes."

He lifts his chin and stares at the ceiling, one hand braced on the sink, the other clutching his crutch, his knuckles turning white as he grips tighter. I watch as he blows out a defeated breath and his voice cracks. "Have you seen her?"

I knew this was coming. It was only a matter of time before he asked about Jana. He hasn't mentioned her name once, even now he can't say it aloud. I hurt for him; unable to imagine his pain. If it doesn't make any sense to me, how can it possibly make any sense to him?

"No, I haven't. She's gone, Colt."

His head turns so fast he nearly loses his balance. "What do you mean she's gone?"

"She's not here anymore."

"Where did she go?" He sounds desperate, as if his air supply is being slowly cut off. I feel as if I'm the one cutting his heart out of his chest.

"Her records have been sealed." I shake my head. "More like expunged, really. I even had your grandpa try to get info. I don't know how she did it, but it's like she never existed here. And if I could do it," I sneer, "I'd do the same for your brain. You're better off."

He shakes his head vehemently, trying to suck air into his lungs as reality starts to get a foothold, but hasn't quite climbed over the wall. "Sebastian, there has to be a reason."

"There is," I mumble, standing to help him get to the sofa as he seems to have lost strength with this news. "You were too fucking good for her."

I help my broken friend hobble to the sofa; a crutch on one side, me on the other. His physical injuries are only a part of his brokenness, his emotional pain is another battle he needs to fight through. For the first time in my life, I see a spirit broken, a soul crushed, a heart ripped in two.

And this is the reason I do what I do. I fuck and go home… before I get fucked and end up alone.

Commitment applies to goals, friends, and end results. Commitment to a woman results in insanity. Case in point: Colton Kinkaid.

I've only met one that made me think with one head over the other, maybe even that heart I claim doesn't exist. *Nina.* Pure, innocent, soft, flawless…a memory. A memory that visits my mind when it gets too crowded with reality. Like an angel visits your dreams; translucent, ethereal, but most of all…untouchable.

Chapter 4

The healing process

"Two miles today," I warn him. "We're not pushing it, Colt."

We're hitting the open track for the first time. Gray is on one side of him, I'm on the other. Colt has been running on the treadmill for the last month. It's been a long, slow process but I'll give the guy credit – he's determined. The more strength he gets back, the more he pushes himself, and the more he pushes himself the stronger he gets. Teaching him to pace himself is a whole different animal. He used to be laid back, easygoing, relaxed, so quick to laugh. I haven't heard Colt laugh since France.

We made it home for Christmas break, stayed for three days, and couldn't wait to get the hell out. Colt ended up staying with me at my folks' house and now we're back in Boston. As we have our own apartment off campus, we don't need to stay away for the entire holiday break and going home leads to tension which is the one thing none of us need.

"Let's start with two and if it goes well, we'll keep going," Colt says.

I shrug and look to Grayson who returns the same defeated

expression to me. Colton suddenly takes off without us.

"You pussies coming or not?" he challenges. I stay behind for a few moments to look for any atrophy in his leg muscles, follow the instructions given me by his physical therapists as closely as I can – due to the dickhead taking off without us – but quite frankly it's easier to observe from a short distance behind.

His gait is excellent, his balance isn't off in the least. His shoulders are straight, hips are aligned, feet aren't too close nor too far apart.

"You done staring at my ass, Chambers?" he yells over his shoulder. "Looks good, doesn't it? Wanna take a bite out of it, don't you? Sorry, pal. I've told you before, I'm just not that into you."

That asshole is goading me…and now I see why. Three gorgeous women standing at the entrance doors to the indoor track; staring, admiring, nearly salivating. And here I am, running a short distance behind Colt…blatantly studying his body, staring at his ass. Sonofabitch!

For the first time since Europe, I see my best friend smile and hear him laughing.

So fucking worth it.

* * *

We all go out for dinner this evening and hit a bar for drinks after. Something clicked on that track today, we got a piece of the old Colton back. It's the first time Colt has had liquor since the accident, and he stops at two whiskeys as do Grayson and I. We watch a football game when we get back home, drink another beer from the six-pack that we purchased on the way, and say goodnight when it's over.

One of these days I'm gonna get laid again, and so is Colton. One way or another, we're going to make him forget her. She will be so long forgotten he won't even remember her name. Watching him go through physical pain is one thing. Watching him fight the emotional pain of losing the love of his life is another. Deep down inside, I know he's still not over it. But once we get him to take that leap, he will be putting cliff divers to shame.

* * *

Classes are back in session after the winter break and the decision was made to no longer have home care and constant keepers in the apartment.

Colt gets around fine on his own – no braces, no walkers, no canes. Every item for assistance with walking has been removed from the apartment and every reminder of the accident has been discarded as well. The cook, housekeeper, and laundry service remain. Why give up a good thing? He hasn't been cleared to drive yet; still battling a little hand-eye coordination skills but improving every day.

"Where are you going?" I ask when I see him coming out of his room early Monday morning – dressed and ready to walk out the door – backpack slung over his right shoulder.

Grayson and I have classes all day, both of us ready to start second semester.

"Class," Colton says casually. "Same place you guys are."

Grayson and I freeze midbite, jaws open, and in unison ask, "What?" It sounds a little more like "whaamp", but he understands.

Colt rolls his eyes. "I signed up for two classes. It's a light load; I can handle it. No time like the present to get back on track."

"Colt, are you sure you want to…"

He shoots me a scathing glare. "Don't. I've got this and you can either let me ride with you or I can call for a ride. What's it going to be?"

Grayson – ever the peacekeeper – shrugs. "Seat's open, Colt. Once you're driving again, you can haul my ass around." He looks up, a huge shit eating grin on his face, his eyes lit with amusement. "Hey! I could get laid in the backseat while you drive me around between clas… damn! That hurt!" He winces, rubbing the back of his head where I've just planted a sharp slap.

"I get the first ride." I narrow my eyes, arching one brow. "In more ways than one."

"It's a nice sized backseat," he protests. "Hell, they could straddle us, side by side. I'll share. There's room."

"Well," Colton says as his lips tip in a smirk. "If that ain't a boner killer, I don't know what is. Grayson's pickle next to your dickle in the backseat going at it next to each other. Think you can carry the same rhythm? Not sure how much stress my suspension can take with uneven rocking." He points his thumb towards the door. "Can we go now?"

I'm not sure Colton realizes his slip. It was a Jana reference to our anatomy; Grayson's 'pickle' and my 'dickle'. She and her friend, Kinzie, used to tease us about how we liked them tickled. If he does, he covers it quickly by turning away and heading for the door. Grayson and I glance at each other, concern etched on our foreheads but silent in voice. We set our silverware down and head for the door – the housekeeper will clean it up. Apparently, we still have some memory cleaning to do.

Chapter 5

Europe All by Myself

"Neither of you want to join me?" I ask. "You're sure?"

We're sitting at a quiet table in the back of our old haunt: the "Tainted" bar. It's been over a year since we've been here – our college hangout after football games – the place where Colton met Jana four years ago. Grayson and I determined it would be another step in the process of memory cleansing; make that bad memory bleaching. Colt needs to be able to go anywhere without being reminded of the ghost of his past. That, and it's a damn fine place to find a quick lay for the night. Gray and I have finished our first year of law school and Colt finished the two classes he took – acing them both.

"Why in hell would I want to go to Europe with you?" Colt asks, his face scrunching in disgust. "We didn't end up backpacking the last time as it was. Two weeks in and we were sucking down wine, eating ourselves into croissant food comas, and you were trying to set a record for the number of lays in a day."

Grayson chuckles. "Sounds like Chambers." He tips his chin and asks, "When are they going to mass produce the Sebastian dildo in your honor?"

I smirk and shake my head. "There is no honor in trying to simulate the real thing, and definitely no replacing it." I sniff and rub a knuckle under my eye, feigning a fallen tear. "They'll have to build a monument in my name when I'm gone where women can go to weep."

Colt groans loudly. "Good God, please go dip your dick and get this over with. If I hear you pound the wall in the shower one more morning, I'm going to send the housekeeper in to bleach it out."

"You guys good to call a driver?" I grin as I tilt my head towards the bar. "I see a redhead over there that looks like she could use some company."

Colt rolls his eyes. "Get out of here. Double wrap it."

"That brunette looks pretty damn good, too," Grayson adds with a bob of his eyebrows. "He did say double wrap, didn't say what to wrap it with."

"Nah, not my type," I tell him. "She's all yours."

I haven't touched a brunette since . . . Nina.

* * *

"You couldn't be happy in Fiji?" Grayson asks before I close the door to his car. He's dropping me at the airport this morning to catch my flight to Paris. "A lot less work stripping off a bikini than…"

"Got it Gray. Thanks for the ride." I slam the door closed and turn to the entrance of the airport. My heart skips a beat as I get closer to the ticket counter. Why am I doing this? I told her not to wait for me. I'm only checking on her, making sure she's safe. Yeah, that's what I'm doing.

* * *

The plane touches down eight hours later in Paris. I didn't sleep the entire flight for thinking about my motives. I tried to offset the anxiety as I flipped through a few law books, read up on new legislation. Surprisingly, it stuck. The more I read, the more ambitious I got to do something different. The desire to work in corporate law took a fast one-eighty as I thought about Colton and what happened – rather what happened immediately after.

Senator Gunde's son, Eaton, was the guilty party for Colton's accident; the drunk driver who hit Colton head-on and nearly killed him; caused him so much pain he nearly killed himself again by way of suicide. Cost him a year of his life recuperating from the damage caused because he got behind the wheel instead of calling for a ride. And what did it cost him? Not a thing. What did it cost his daddy? A shit ton of money that Colton's parents agreed to in lieu of charges against Eaton. What did it do for me? Loathe Colt's parents even more. Colt was so far out of it for too long before he could do anything and Briggs was only durable POA, so his hands were tied at the time. Since Gunde lost his senate seat this past year, I have the feeling Briggs did manage to cause damage; I'm just not sure how. Gunde is now a has-been in the political and corporate world. Couldn't have happened to a nicer guy. *See what I did there?*

Being prosecuting attorneys isn't going to make us jack, but let's be honest; we've got plenty of money, none of us need jack. Give us a Jill a couple times a week to keep our dicks warm and we're happy. *Don't judge.*

* * *

I find the café without any difficulty the next day. I took the evening and night to adjust to the jet lag, though six hours isn't that difficult to adjust to when age is still on your side and anxiety fuels your stamina.

Standing across the street, I take in the activities on the patio and watch as she waits the tables – much like I did before I left last year. She's still as beautiful; if not more so. Definitely more so, I think after only a few moments. She wears her white blouse, black pants, apron tied at her waist, sensible shoes. Her hair is tied back in a long ponytail.

She sets drinks and lunch on a table for a couple patrons before she hesitates and glances around, but I'm hidden today. I made sure to stay out of sight – obscured from her view while keeping her in mine – but it's easy to see she's now distracted. A soft smile encompasses her mouth as she turns to go back inside. I stay planted where I am, waiting for her to return. When she does, her hands are empty, saving a large piece of paper with bold letters that she holds high so I can read it:

"Je sais que tu es ici, S`ebastien". I know you are here, Sebastian.

I step out from the shadows, a smile on my face, slowly shaking my head. She felt it, she knew. I make my way across the street as she rounds the gate yard closure to the patio and jumps into my arms. Why I suddenly feel like I'm home, I'll never know, but I do.

"Watch a sunset with me tonight?" I whisper as I hold her tight.

"If you'll count the stars with me," she whispers back.

"Nina," I murmur. I haven't spoken her name aloud in a year and it feels like a cool drink on my dry throat.

"S`ebastien," she says with a smile that lights up her face. "I'm done at six."

"I'll be here." I set her back on her feet, place a kiss on her forehead and walk away, leaving what feels like the best part of me behind.

* * *

"It's been a challenging year," I tell her.

"He's lucky to have people like you in his life," she says. "Not everyone has that."

Nina brought us to the same place we were last year – on the banks of the Seine. The blanket is beneath us. I brought the same wine, cheese, bread and grapes. She drank wine last year, so I took my chances. It's iffy here; presence of adults law and all.

"Physically, he's healing. But he's still broken on the inside and I can't fix it. He lost the love of his life," I sigh. "He hasn't been the same since."

She leans her head on my shoulder and rubs my arm. "She may have been the love of his life, but if he wasn't the love of hers, he didn't lose her, she lost him. I can only dream of being the love of someone's life. I think maybe in the end, he won."

I'd never thought to explain it that way to Colt; at least not that eloquently. When I get back, maybe I can try Nina's words and see if they sink in any better; make him realize he's the winner. They wanted kids someday. What if it had happened then?

I hold her closer to me, relishing the warmth of her body next to mine. She fits so perfectly under my arm. "You are wise beyond your years."

"I am more things that wise beyond my years, S`ebastien," she whispers, nuzzling her mouth against my neck; kissing, nipping. "I waited for you."

"Nina," I groan. "We can't. I can't."

"It feels like you can," she teases as she reaches for my crotch, revealing a prominent hardness aching for what I know deep down inside I cannot have. I want her, yes, but I won't let her become a conquest. I like what we have; it's different, special. And she's so…innocent, and I like the innocence.

"You don't want me?" She sounds hurt as she pulls away to the other side of the blanket and sighs.

"I want you," I do my best to explain. "But you're not mine to have. Not like that."

"How do you want me, S`ebastien?" she whispers, a tear falling down her cheek.

"With my hands, my mouth." I reach to wipe her tears away. "Prove to me I have a heart, Nina," I plead. "Don't let me walk away with your virtue. You're too young, and I'm not worth it."

"What happens to me when you find someone else?"

The very thought nearly makes me laugh. "Nina, look at me." I tilt her chin up, forcing her eyes to meet mine. "I've never trusted anyone with my heart before you."

She narrows her eyes, testing me. "What if someone else

wants mine?"

"Give it to them," I tell her honestly. "They're more worthy than I am."

Her eyes rim with tears and the words she speaks will forever echo in my mind. *"Mon couer t`appartient, S`ebastien."* My heart belongs to you.

"I don't deserve it, Nina." I gather the things from the blanket and start to pack them in the basket. When the last item is packed away, she moves to straddle me.

"I will decide who gets my heart, S`ebastien Chambers," she chides as she holds my chin in a firm grip. "I will decide if you are worth it or not and I will prove to you that you have a heart."

"Nina…"

She stops me with a kiss planted firmly on my mouth, her hands pulling at my hair while they pull me closer to her at the same time. I hear the growl in my throat, feel the rumble in my chest as I wrap her hair in my fist and tug gently, taking control of the kiss, lost in the power of knowing she'll succumb to my whims. Old habits die hard.

For the first time in my life, my senses overrule my physical need and wants as I break the kiss, my breathing uneven and stuttered. "Nina…no!" I lean my forehead on hers, placing my palms on her cheeks. "I can't. I will ruin you."

"I'm sorry," she whispers.

"I'm sorry too," I return, gently lifting her off my lap and standing.

"Just spend time with me, Bast," she says, pleading. "I promise I won't ask more. I need you in my life."

"I need you in mine, too." More than she will ever know, I think. I reach for her hand and pull her to her feet. I hold her in my arms and relish the feel of her body close to mine; the warmth and the closeness of what I want but can't have. The self-restraint I've never had to subject myself to. She deserves better but I can't cut her loose completely. She's like a lifeline that keeps me afloat in stormy waters that I tend to swim in. I'm a shark in a sea of helpless guppies that feeds on physical needs and exits while the sheets are warm, leaving a cold spot for the women to wake up to. I never fix them breakfast. I'm out the door before they can say 'good morning'. Most of the time, I don't even know their names.

She lifts her chin and gazes into my eyes. "Sunsets and stars?"

I smile and nod. "I think we can do a cappuccino or two as well."

Two weeks later I leave – Nina's virtue intact – that thing in my chest beating a little harder, softened even more for the girl who stole it the year before.

Chapter 6

It's official: Grayson Kibbey has lost his fucking mind

"You what?!" I ask, rounding the sofa, going to the kitchen to fill my glass with another tall shot of whiskey.

Colt is out of the apartment at the present time, visiting his parents – God knows why– probably to hear his mother tell him once again why he should hate Jana. We already know why he should hate Jana! Why he has the incessant need to be reminded, I'll never know, but he feeds on it; needing to hear the story now and again of how she left him in his time of need.

"We…it just happened, Seb. I can't explain it," he says.

"Try me," I sneer, on the verge of sending a fist to his face. This could be a major setback for Colt. He's come so far, and we're supposed to be a team – the three Amigos – and Grayson's betrayal feels like he's just pissed on the parade of success. He is now dating Jana's best friend from college. A literal lineup of pussy out there and he has to hook up with one that could undo a year's worth of work.

"We just…she's fun. I've never met anyone like her," he stammers, struggling to find the right words. "We click. We fit."

"You fit?" I laugh bitterly. "Better than the usual pussy you slide into?"

"Knock it off!" he yells. "I won't have you talking about my girl that way."

"Your girl?" I laugh sarcastically. "How long has this been going on, Gray? Of all the pussy in Boston, you gotta pick…"

"Enough!" he shouts. "Kinzie and I are solid, like it or not. And you will treat her with respect. I don't care if you approve. I'm not asking."

"And where does Jana fit in this?" I ask. "Are they still buddies, best friends? Think she'll be bringing her over for threesomes?" I scowl, picturing the repercussions. "Nice work, Gray. This ought to be real good for Colt."

"She and Jana haven't been in contact since graduation," he says, shaking his head. "She has no idea what happened to her. And Kinz is just as pissed about what happened as any of us!"

Lost in our conversation – aka shouting match – neither one of us has noticed Colton enter the apartment.

"Colt," I greet him, high hopes that he hasn't heard much, if anything.

"Hope I'm not interrupting anything," he says, his eyes narrowed as he glances back and forth between us.

"Uh, we were just…" I stutter.

"Don't mind me," he mumbles, heading towards his room.

"Colt, you want to go…" Grayson fumbles.

"Nope." He slams his door shut.

"Fan-fucking-tastic," I growl. "Two steps forward, three steps back." I glare at Grayson. "And to think, it only took a year. Get somebody else to tickle your pickle, Kibbey. Don't bring her around here."

"Fuck you, Chambers. It's my place too. He needs to move on and Kinzie is not Jana." He sets his glass down so hard it shatters on the counter. "Clean it up yourself. I'm outta here." He slams the door so hard on his way out a picture frame falls off the wall, landing with a thunk followed by the sound of breaking glass.

I stand at the counter watching whiskey leak onto the floor, the shards of glass having made their way onto the floor as well. I stare at Colt's closed door; wondering how long it's going to be this time before it opens and he enters the land of the living.

He didn't lose her; she lost him. Nina's words. Worth a shot.

As I clean up the mess Grayson made, I hear Colt's door open.

He makes his way past me to the fridge, opening the door and taking out a water. He chugs half the bottle before he leans against the fridge and sighs. "We can't help who we fall in love with, Sebastian."

"Wouldn't know anything about that," I mumble. *Yeah, I'm a liar.*

"Consider yourself lucky." He slaps my shoulder on his way out of the kitchen.

"Hey, Colt."

He pauses, his back to me. "Yeah?"

"Have you ever stopped to think you can't lose what you never had?" I pause, fighting for the perfect words. "It's not just about them being the love of your life, but you being theirs too."

I look up as he turns around and I shrug. "I don't know, man. I just wouldn't want to spend my life with somebody knowing I want them more than they want me. You were going to put a ring on her, Colt. That in sickness and in health shit? Better you found out when you did." My mouth twists and I blow out a breath. "I don't think you lost; I think she did. Because she is never going to find what she had with you."

He nods slowly. "You're right, she's not. And I am never going to be that stupid again." A look in his eyes I haven't seen in years takes hold and he smiles slyly. "What do you say we head to the classier side of the city tonight and relieve a little pent-up tension?"

I match his smile and agree wholeheartedly. "I'd say it's just what the doctor ordered, and we don't even need a prescription."

He tips his chin and smirks. "Just be sure to double wrap it so you don't need one after."

"You need to grab some condoms out of my nightstand?

Got plenty," I offer.

He looks at me like I offered him dirty socks. "Oh please," he says, rolling his eyes. "I need something to fit my dick, not my index finger."

I snort, enjoying the banter. "Fuck you, Kinkaid."

"I've been fucked plenty, Sebastian." He lifts his brow. "It's my turn. You can have my leftovers."

He actually left the bar with a woman that night. Don't have a clue what happened. We didn't talk about it. He went one way; I went another. His was a redhead…mine was a blonde.

This second year of law school is definitely going to be easier than the first.

Chapter 7

"Make the punishment fit the crime"

"How would you guys feel about changing the type of law we practice?" We're sitting around the dining table at home eating pizza and drinking a couple beers. I had asked if we could order in tonight so we could talk. You would think by the looks on their faces when I'd asked they thought I was going to break the news I was dying…or moving out.

Grayson's head drops back as he stares at the ceiling and he blows out a breath. "That's all this is? You're not somebody's baby daddy? You're not transferring to Stanford?"

"Baby daddy? Stanford? Just a minute." I hold up one finger, grab my bottle of beer, chug what's left in it, swish a bit in my mouth, swallow and release a huge belch. "Ahhh…yeah. Had to wash that shit out of my mouth. Pizza the second time around with a hint of sour beer definitely tasted better." I glare at Grayson. "Are you nuts?! I double wrap for a reason and I'm on a roll here to finish early with honors."

"Well, what were we supposed to think?" He stares at me, his mouth agape. He holds his arms wide, palms up. "Pizza and beer at home. I thought maybe you were sick, dying even."

"We're all dying, Grayson. Eventually we…"

He grabs his hair with both hands and pulls. "Oh shit. You are dying, aren't you? You won't be in my wedding and…"

Colt and I turn to him and in unison ask, "Your what?"

His eyes flit back and forth between us before he grimaces. "Oh, oh yeah. I was meaning to talk to you about that."

"Oh, oh yeah," I snidely mimic him. "I'm sure you were."

"Sebastian, knock it off," Colt warns. "We've been over this. Gray, we'll get to you in a minute. Chambers, what is it you had to say?"

Grayson getting married is not going to deter my goals, but it might change my thoughts on a partnership. Maybe little Miss Kinzie won't be amenable to a change in plans, and she'll fly away as fast as Jana did – one can only hope. And if Grayson doesn't want to climb on board, maybe now is the time for him to make plans for something else.

"I don't want to practice corporate law," I tell them.

Silence.

"Okay," Colt says quietly, studying the beer bottle in front of him.

Gray's brows are furrowed as he presses his fingers to his temples.

With more conviction for anything I've ever felt in my life, I announce, "I want to prosecute. No more slaps on the wrist, no more community service. I want jail time, convictions, loss of luxuries." I look Colton straight in the eyes as I finish the last words and say, "And repercussions for the crimes committed no matter who they are or how much money their daddy has."

Colt's expression is clouded with confusion and pain until I watch his eyes gloss over with the slightest film of tears. And then I see it: gratitude. It's not what I was looking for. No, I was hoping to see a fire in them that screamed revenge. He'll get there, I tell myself. *Baby steps. She ripped his heart out.*

Grayson groans so loudly, I fear any passersby in the hall might hear him. "Good God, I thought you were dying. Then I thought you were quitting." He gets up to get more beer from the fridge. He slaps me across the back of the head when he returns. "You asshole. Why didn't you just say you want to right the wrongs of the world? Jesus, such a drama queen."

"So, you're on board?" I ask, rubbing my scalp, forgiving the slap just this once.

"Of course I'm on board," he says. "Eaton Gunde shouldn't be on a damn bicycle let alone behind the wheel of a car." He sets down two more beers on the table after popping the tops; and holds his up in cheers. "To the newest bad ass attorneys in Vermont. Here we come."

Colt scrunches his nose in disgust. "Bad ass attorneys. B-A-A. Sounds like sheep. *Baaahhh.* Nope. Gonna need a better acronym."

"Bad ass lawyers," Grayson quips, snapping his fingers. "B-A-L. Balls."

"If you're missing a testicle," I snarl.

"Ah come on," he pleads. "We gotta come up with something." He snaps his fingers again. "B-A-D. Bad ass dudes. Bad ass dicks?"

Colt and I both slump in our chairs, heads in our hands, groaning.

"You're only going to be dipping yours in one valley, Kibbey," I remind him. "Nothing to boast about."

He heaves a sigh before he murmurs, "I really love her, guys."

Looking up at him, all I see is this sappy, longing man who has been dragged into the depths of hell. But that's my skeptic self. Because with all that sappy longing I see a glint of happiness I hate to admit looks pretty damn good on Grayson Kibbey. It softens the hard edges, releases that tic in his jaw. The mere mention of Kinzie puts a smile on his face that makes me want to roll my eyes. But it's also everything I seem to feel when I'm in Europe. When I'm with *Nina.* Looking at him now and being reminded of Nina, I feel that damn organ between my throat and my belly skip a beat. She's my secret and I plan to keep it that way. I don't let them see that soft side of me, the part that could be broken.

Colton smiles. "We're happy for you, Grayson." I see the warning in his eyes as he prompts me, "Aren't we?"

"We are," I reply, patting his shoulder.

"I need you both to be my best man." He shakes his head. "I'm not choosing between the two of you."

Colt shrugs. "As long as Sebastian wears the dress, I'm good with it. I'll be happy to escort him down the aisle."

I scowl. "Funny man, Kinkaid."

He shrugs again and grins. "Shave your legs, smile pretty, lipstick, nobody will know. The ladies always said you liked wearing lingerie."

"It was college, and I stuffed their panties in my pocket as keepsakes!"

True story.

They laugh loudly. "Yeah, if I remember correctly, that was quite a drawerful you had by the time you were done collecting," Grayson says.

I narrow my eyes and remind him, "It was a dresser full. And after having them laundered and repackaged, the women's shelter was quite appreciative of the donation." I begin to gather bottles from the table and rise to put them in the recycling bin. "So, when is the happy occasion?" They follow, carrying items from the table as well.

"Not until after graduation." Gray deposits the items he's carrying in the trash and brushes his hands off. "I'm okay with a long engagement and Kinz is in no hurry. We know we're solid. That's all that matters."

"Cool, that'll give us plenty of time to talk you out of… son of a bitch!" I yell, bending in pain and tumbling to my left as Colton jabs his elbow into my side. I glare at him and he scowls.

"What?" I grunt, holding my side. "I was going to say talk him out of having a big wedding!"

Total lie.

"Of course you were." He smirks. "That's always your first thought when a friend announces he's getting married…right after 'does she have a sister for me'?"

I visibly shudder at the very thought and mutter, "I'd use my own hand first."

"We know," he teases. "You already do. We've heard. Who's Nina by the way?"

"What?" My head turns so fast, I pull a muscle and wince as I rub the back of my neck. There's no way they've heard anything. One: I don't beat off in the shower – I don't need to. Two: I've never said her name aloud…ever.

"You called out her name when you fell asleep on the sofa the other night. Just figured she must have been memorable." He chuckles. "Should we check your dresser drawer for panties?"

"No panties in the drawer, Colt. Must have been memorable somehow though," I tell him, forcing a laugh. "Too bad it's only in my dreams. Think I might head out tonight and refresh my memory. You in?" I ask, reaching for my coat from the hook by the door. It's my MO: distracting myself with members of the female persuasion. It's easy; mechanical and physical. They get off, I get off, I go home, and they fix their own breakfast. I'm just not that guy.

"I'm gonna pass tonight," he replies, frowning. "Not up to it."

Grayson Kibbey will end up a statistic…they always do.

Chapter 8

"It's the lattes and croissants, I swear"

"You're going back again?" Colt asks, pacing himself after a five-mile run this morning. It has become our daily routine with the exception of Sundays. "Is there something specific about France or is the pussy that much better?" I fight to keep my eyes from rolling. It's my two weeks of the year dedicated to celibacy and he thinks I'm going there to get laid. I could get laid here anytime.

"You can always go with me, find out for yourself," I offer. I know he isn't able to go; he's taking extra classes this summer, trying to catch up from his missed year of school. One more year for Kibbey and me and we're done. Pass the bar exam and the shingle goes up. Colt will have a little longer before he's done, but he's working his ass off to get there. If it weren't for Nina, I'd love to have him join me. I specifically chose this time so he couldn't. Call me an asshole, go ahead. It's not going to make me feel any worse than I already do.

"Maybe next year. I'll be better fit for backpacking." He slows for our final walk around the track.

He could go with me this year. His limp only appears when he gets too tired. He's out of physical therapy, he runs like a jackal.

The winter is harder on him than any other time of year because of the bone damage he suffered in the accident. He's come a long way in the last couple years, but the accident gave him a hard edge. He's bitter, still angry, and his sense of humor is dry. I overheard one of the women he'd been with make the comment in a bar a few weeks ago that "he fucks like a demon". *At least there's that.*

I, myself, blame Jana for his pain. I see it in his eyes, I hear it in his voice. He still calls out her name in his sleep for God's sake. And the worst part? It's not anger I hear. No, it's desire and pleasure; always ending in pain. I hate that woman for what she did to him; for ruining the best part of my friend – his heart.

"If I chose another place, would you go with me?" My brow lifts. "Somewhere tropical, full of bikinis?"

He lets out a slow sad laugh and stops, his breaths becoming slow and even. "You think this has to do with her?"

"Does it?"

He shakes his head slowly and sighs. "No, there's apparently a reason you need to go back and there are reasons I need to stay."

"The accident?"

He blows out a deep frustrated breath. "Sebastian, I'm seeing somebody, okay?"

My jaw drops open and I blink fast. "You're seeing somebody? You didn't tell me?" I bob my eyebrows and grin. "Is she hot?"

He smirks. "She is a he."

"Whoa…" I reply, drawing it out much longer than I intended. "Okay. This is a bit of a surprise. I mean, um, if that's how you are. If it's how you really feel, uh…I had no idea." I scratch the back of my head, cheeks flushed, lost for words. Huh… who woulda thunk it?

He stands with his arms crossed; a smirk pulls his mouth to the side as he rolls his eyes. He reaches out and slaps me upside the head. "Are you finished now, dumbass? I'm seeing a therapist twice a week. His name is Dr. Michael Collins." He shakes his head and laughs. "Told you before, I'm just not that into you."

He starts walking toward the exit and I follow quickly

behind. "Colt, if you were, you know…" I wave my hands, embarrassed. "I'd be okay with it…I-I wouldn't hold it against you."

He shoots a disgusted glance at my crotch and back up to my face, grimacing. "Chambers, you ever hold that thing against me, I'll chop it off and serve it to you for breakfast. I know where it's been."

Maybe he does know he calls out her name in his sleep. Maybe the doc can fix what Grayson and I couldn't.

My plane lands late evening – giving me the opportunity to get settled, get some sleep and be rested and on time to see Nina working at the café the next day. It dawns on me as I walk the now familiar sidewalk that I'm taking a lot for granted. What if she doesn't work here anymore? We have no way to keep in touch – we have never exchanged phone numbers or addresses. We have no communication in the year that passes between my trips here. I do think I could find her neighborhood – the 17th arrondissement – but who's to say she still lives there? And which apartment does she live in? My heart races faster as I hasten my footsteps to the spot I plan to stand while I observe her once again. What if I never find her? What if she has given her heart to someone else? My stomach plummets as thoughts race through my head. What have I done?

Suddenly my world calms. I can breathe. My heartbeat slows, my hands stop shaking, my stomach stops roiling. I can feel the roots of my hair stop tingling as it relaxes against my scalp. She's here. I watch as she delivers a tray of pastries and cups of coffee to a table of patrons.

My God, she's beautiful.

She's taller, her breasts are a little fuller, cheekbones more defined. I feel my fingers twitch and itch as they long to reach out to touch her; caress her silky skin, tuck her hair behind her ear. I long to hear her say my name. *Saybastyaun.* Nobody says it like Nina. And she calls me Bast. Either one makes me smile.

She disappeared inside the café minutes ago and hasn't returned. There is other wait staff tending to the tables she was before. I start to worry that something's happened. Did her shift end? Did she get hurt and can't come back out? Why can't I see her?

I feel familiar hands reach from behind as they slowly wrap around my rib cage and hug me. Her scent fills my nostrils and I breathe deep to capture my favorite aroma. *Nina.* I feel her cheek rest high between my shoulder blades as her breasts press against my back.

"Watch a sunset with me?" she whispers.

"Only if we can watch the stars come out after," I whisper back.

I spin around, pick her up and hold her close as she wraps her legs around my waist.

"Nina." I breathe her name like it's air to a drowning man – because it is.

"S`ebastien," she whispers softly.

"Say it again."

Her smile takes my breath away as she gazes into my eyes and says my name once more. "S`ebastien."

My favorite flavor, my favorite sensation, my favorite everything comes together as our mouths seal in a kiss that I've waited for since I left her a year ago. How am I ever going to leave it again in two weeks? *Be strong, Chambers. This is a fix. She's a Band-Aid. Symptomatic treatment, not a cure. Rehab for a sex addict.*

"I am eighteen now, Bast," she says as her eyes light up. "I have been for six months." I know that look and I know what she's thinking. While Nina's eyes hold innocence and enthusiasm to learn and explore, the women back home would be licking their lips, grabbing my crotch, and purring while offering head in exchange for a good ride. And that is the difference between Nina and the world I live in. She's my escape from that and I cannot let something so delicate be tainted and stained by someone like me. She deserves better.

"And even more beautiful than you were when I saw you last," I murmur, not bothering to add still untouchable – we'll get to that later. I just need this moment. She feels so good in my arms, her smile so warm and welcoming, eyes that I could gaze into for hours and never grow tired. A laugh that I want to hear for the rest of my... Stop! There is no rest of my life here…unless I get hit by a bus before I leave.

"Maybe we can watch a sun*rise* together this time?" she suggests shyly, fiddling with the collar on shirt. "I waited for you, S`ebastien."

"Pick you up at six?' I ask, smiling though clearly avoiding the subject. "Same sunset as last time?"

She looks disappointed – I swear she can read my mind – but masks it quickly and nods. "Same stars too." She kisses me again and hugs my neck after. "I missed you, S`ebastien."

I squeeze her tighter, relishing the feel of her body against mine. We fit so well. "I missed you too, Nina." I know I need to set her back on her feet so she can finish work and meet me later. I know she needs to walk away, if only for a few hours. We'll be back together in a little while. So why can I not let go? Why can I not unbury my face from the crook of her neck, her scent, the soft skin that I caress with my mouth? Why? Because it feels like home – that's why.

She rubs her core against my stomach and moans, "S`ebastien." Shit! She's grinding against my belt buckle and I'm the one who caused it. Dry humping in the middle of the sidewalk in Paris. It happens, right?

I carefully lift her up a few inches – so she doesn't get scraped on my belt buckle – then set her down on her feet. Her cheeks are flushed and some of her hair has fallen out of its ponytail. She's frustrated and breathing heavily, her fists clenched at her sides. I'm nearly anticipating a foot stomp, but Nina is not a petulant child. She's more mature than most of the women I bed back in the states, and those women are satisfied customers. I gently place my hands on her shoulders and lean my forehead on hers.

"You should get back to work. I'll pick you up at six," I say softly. I touch my lips to her forehead and leave a kiss.

Her head is down as she walks away towards the café

across the street; dejected, embarrassed; probably a bit horny too. She stops walking when I call out her name.

"I really did miss you." I see her nod; her chin lifts higher, and her shoulders straighten as she resumes walking. The throb in my own pants reminds me I'm not an innocent party in any of this. I've never said I didn't want her – I simply know I can't have her. She deserves so much better.

This trip is going to require a helluva lot of cold showers. I stare at my right hand and flex my fingers. 'Hello, old friend', I think. Desperate times call for desperate measures. She may want it – I can't have it.

* * *

"Let's walk the beach first." I'm out of the car and closing my door before she has a chance to protest. I will not take Nina back to my hotel room. I know my limits, my ability to maintain self-control – I have none.

While I know Nina needs release, I need relief. I come here to get away from it all. Away from the cold harshness that is my world, the meaningless sex that makes me feel relaxed until I'm ready to bed the next one. The nameless, faceless romps that satisfy me physically, never fulfilling anything but an animalistic desire. I'm the wolf that doesn't dress in sheep's clothing because I don't take innocent victims; it's mutual, casual, fun, and never involves cuddling…or breakfast.

I spent the time away from Nina this afternoon crafting a plan that might work for both of us. I'll help her explore, help her learn, but I will not break a barrier that puts the nail in a coffin and buries the one pure thing in my life. I need Nina, for as long as I can have her. This may very well be the last time I can touch innocence and leave it innocent, whole, unscathed and intact – knowing for once it wasn't me responsible for taking what wasn't mine to have.

She's my conscience.

We walk hand-in-hand, in silence; the sand between our toes as the sun sets on the horizon, the rest of the world a mere afterthought. The beach has cleared from the sunbathers and swimmers, leaving a few stragglers who walk the water's edge admiring the sunset.

Nina wears a long white flowing skirt and gauze top that make her look like an angel. The breeze causes the material to blow between her legs and wrap around her body which captures every curve. If it were wet, it would be see-thru. Worse yet, she's braless – as are most of the women in France – but somehow it's only something I notice. It's not something I drool over like I would back in the states. *I'm such a liar. I've surreptitiously wiped my mouth at least a dozen times since I picked her up.* Her hair is down – thick, straight and shiny – the light of the sun highlighting individual strands as it blows in the breeze.

I finally open the conversation. "This year can't be any different than last, Nina."

She sighs as her shoulders sag. "I waited for you, Bast. Just like I said I would."

We stop walking and I take her hands in mine. "I told you not to wait. I'm no good for you."

"Then why did you come back?" she whispers.

"Because you're good for me," I answer, pulling her to me, placing a kiss on her forehead as I stare out at the water. "And because I'm a selfish bastard."

She places her hand over my chest and follows with her cheek right above it. "I hear it beating. You have a heart, S`ebastien. That is the best part of you. Leave me with something this year and I will wait for more. Teach me. That is all I ask."

She stands on her tiptoes, wraps her hands around my neck and pulls my mouth to hers. Her body literally melts into mine and mine into hers. She plays with the ends of my hair, her touch so soft it sends tingles down my spine. No aggression, no demands; just sweetness and light. She's so much more a woman now than she was two years ago, but she will always be the one I can't have... the one I can't ruin.

"We'll walk some more," she says as she pulls away from the kiss. "We have a sunset to watch, S`ebastien Chambers."

We come to the end of the beach where the woods start, leading to the rocky cliffs ahead. The sun hasn't set yet – the orange sky casting a dusky glow – but we're nearing dark. The beach is deserted at this end, no one in sight.

"We should probably head back." I tug on her hand gently, turning back in the direction of the car.

"Not yet," she says.

"It's getting dark."

She giggles. "I know. Sit with me," she orders as she plops down in the sand. "We'll take a rest."

"Nina, it's getting dark," I protest. "We'll never find our way back."

"Yes we will," she reassures me with a laugh. "We have flashlights on our phones, and I know the way. I promise."

I shrug off my hoodie and take my seat in the sand next to her. I turn toward her and ask, "What do we need a rest fro…" *Whoa!*

Her blouse is unbuttoned, and she swings her leg over my lap until she's straddling me, her skirt rising to her thighs as she does. "You don't have to give me you, S`ebastien. I will give you me. Teach me. Show me something."

Her blouse hangs open, breasts in full view. She's perfect, more so than I had fantasized. The backdrop of the sunset nearing its end – the moonlight soon to appear – only enhances the sight before me. I can give her something; just not everything. And if we get caught? At least she's legal.

She's rubbing herself against me once again, desperate for friction and relief.

"Patience," I whisper, lifting my thighs to boost her up so she has nothing but open air touching her center. She whimpers softly. "Ssshhh," I hush her, wrapping my fingers in her hair, bringing her mouth to mine in a slow languorous kiss. I feel the weight of her breast in my hand as I slowly massage it and gently tug on her nipple. She gasps and shivers before she arches her back, grasps the back of my head and moves my mouth to her nipple.

"S`ebastien," she moans as her hips move, fighting to find

their way back to humping ground. "More."

My hand slides up her silky thigh, reaching to slide panties to the side that I now find are nonexistent. *Holy shit!* She's so soft, wet, ready. *Silk.* I use one finger while circling her clit with my thumb. I had planned on adding another but…it's all it takes.

"*Bast…*" she whimpers as she clenches around my finger. She's not a screamer, no dramatics to boost my ego; just a soft descent from being sated. She collapses forward, her body spent – her nipple in my mouth a pleasant memory – her forehead rests on mine. I slowly remove my finger, brushing against her sensitive front as I do, and I feel her tighten and hear her quick intake of breath.

"Thank you," she whispers, a single tear from each eye falls down her cheeks. "Don't hate me, S`ebastien."

"Never, Nina," I murmur before kissing her like the lifeline she is.

I deliver her back home – same as last year and the year before: the 17th arrondissement – after eating our picnic dinner and watching the stars come out. I was smarter this year, having gotten the exact address and apartment number plugged in my GPS. There is no discomfort or awkward conversation after what happened. Okay, that's a lie. There is discomfort but it's behind my zipper and it's only my own; my problem – blue balls. Not the first time and probably not the last. I'll survive.

* * *

Two weeks later, I'm on my way back to the states. A thousand kisses, multiple orgasms for Nina, endless explorations, thirteen sunsets, a million stars, bottomless cups of cappuccinos, and the certain knowledge I must have a heart – because the pain in my chest makes it hard to breathe. Once again Nina's virtue is intact. My sanity may be on edge, but I held true to my vow of celibacy. She wanted to know how to use her hands, her mouth – how to please me. But I'll be damned if I was going to give her lessons or let her use me for practice, knowing those skills would eventually be enjoyed by another man. No, this trip was all about Nina. My right hand may never be able to hold a pen or type again, but if it can grip a beer mug or a glass of whiskey, I'll be fine.

I am headed back into one more year of hell and hard work before passing the bar exam and moving my ass back to Vermont. Colt is going to have a few extra months to spend in Boston, but when that is over, the real hell starts. The difference? The hell won't be for us. It will be for the likes of Eaton Gunde.

We can't keep it from happening, but we can keep it from happening . . . twice.

Chapter 9

The End of An Era, or an Eaton

It took me all of two nights to be back here; my regular drinking establishment, my regular table. I need to get her out of my system; be it by way of redhead, blonde, or hell, I'll even take the one with purple strands weaved through it right now. Anything to get off…the one-way track my mind has been riding. The condoms packed in my wallet are burning a hole in my ass cheek.

"How was Europe?" Colt asks, setting his glass back on the table.

I shrug casually, eyeing the blonde at the end of the bar. "Not bad. It's got its…" I grin as I arch a brow. "…charms."

"Charms." He chuckles. "Is that what they're calling them these…"

"Guys!" Grayson calls out as rushes into the bar. His face is flushed, hair mussed like he's been running his hands through it. He struggles to get through groups of people on his way to our table and bumps shoulders with a few, neglecting to excuse himself as he always does. *Very unlike Grayson.*

"Quite the bedhead you got going there, Gray." I smirk. "Need a comb?"

He rakes his hands through his hair again and tugs at the roots, shifting from foot to foot. His eyes are wide and he looks nervous as his eyes flit from Colt's to mine.

"What do you think, Colt?" I tease as I eye Gray from his head to his toes. "He fell off the wagon of monogamy and has a sudden case of guilt? Does he have to piss, or has he gotten cold feet?"

Colt makes a scrupulous assessment of the man standing at our tableside. "I think he needs a drink. Unless of course she's knocked up. If that's the case, he needs a minivan and a car seat."

"Can I get a drink?" he asks, raking his hands through his hair once more, heaving a deep sigh. He drops himself into a chair next to Colt. "I think we'd better get refills for you guys, too."

I hold up my hand for the waitress, capturing her attention, and hold up three fingers, indicating drinks for all of us. She nods and heads toward the bar.

Now that Grayson has taken a seat and his breaths have slowed, his ashen complexion is obvious. His face is drawn, his mouth twists as he studies his hands.

I furrow my brow and ask, "What's going on, Kibbey?"

"Eaton Gunde decided to go drinking and driving again. He's dead."

In unison Colt and I turn and ask, "What?"

The waitress stops at the table and sets three shots of whiskey in front of us. Before she can turn around and leave, I look up and tell her, "Better bring another round."

I grab my glass and hold it up. "I say we make a cheers."

Grayson sinks back into his chair, shaking his head. "Not so fast, Chambers. He killed two people this time."

Colt's head drops toward his chest as he groans. "Fuck." He raises his head slowly and his voice is but a whisper as he asks Grayson, "Who?"

Grayson swallows hard and winces. "A young couple on their way home from their honeymoon."

My stomach churns as the ire builds. Eaton Gunde was a waste of air and space. He had caused so much damage to Colton;

set him back so far we didn't know if he'd ever move ahead. But now, that wasted space has taken two lives that they're loved ones can never get back. I would love nothing more than to go after Eaton's father; the asshole who got him off the first time. The hush money he paid. More than that though? It reminds me how much I hate Colton's parents for agreeing to it. For being partly responsible for this new tragedy.

See how it all ties together? When you tell one lie, you have to tell another to cover up the first one. Then another to cover that one, then another, and another…

The waitress brings the second round and sets them on the table.

"Pick up your glasses," I tell them as I reach for my own. I watch as they reach for the first shot and then hold up my own. "To one less piece of shit walking the face of the earth." I throw mine back and swallow hard, releasing a harsh breath when I finish. They do the same.

I point to the second shots sitting in front of them and nod. "Now those."

They pick them up and we all hold our glasses up in a toast. "To the couple who lost their lives due to that piece of shit. May they rest in peace together. And to us, the ones who are going to put the inevitable pieces of shit away. To winning."

We tip our glasses toward each other before we shoot them back and swallow.

I look to Colt and see the pain in his eyes. Is it the accident, the aftermath, survivor's guilt? Or is it still Jana? Damn her!

"You made it," I growl, pointing a finger for emphasis. "For a reason. Make it count, Kinkaid."

"I'm gonna get going," Grayson says. "I thought you guys should know. I just found out from my mom and headed over as fast as I could."

"Thanks, Gray," Colton says with a tip of his chin. "I appreciate it."

Grayson nods. "I figured it'd be better coming from me than hearing it on the news."

"You were right," Colt replies. "It sucks from any source, but I would rather have heard it from you."

"You gonna be okay?" His brows furrow. "I know it brings up a lot of bad memories for you, but…" He sighs and tilts his head toward the door. "Kinz is driving and waiting in the car. She thought it would be best if she…"

"I'm good, Gray," he says, shaking his head. I see him subconsciously clench and unclench his fist. "Tell Kinzie hello." *And there we have it. Kinzie…leads to…Jana.*

"Will do." He nods. "Goodnight, guys."

"I thought you and Kinzie were best buds," I comment after Gray has made his way out the door.

He shrugs. "Kinzie and I do fine. She's just easier in small doses." He wrinkles his nose. "Know what I mean?"

"Micro doses," I agree. "And even that's too much some days. I do it for Gray's sake in the name of friendship. He has to live with her, I only have to tolerate her. I was really hoping he had cold feet." I laugh.

He laughs as well. "Your poor mother is going to spend the rest of her days searching for a wife for you. You know that don't you? She'll be on her deathbed crying for little Sebastians or Sebastianettes."

"Not gonna happen," I groan. "I declared myself a baby-free zone a long time ago. The football field, remember?"

"I hope you wrap it in Europe as well as you claim you do here." He grins and winks. "Can't wait to meet little Jean Pierre someday."

The very mention of travel does something to my insides. The subject of the conversation had actually taken my mind somewhere else for a while. It may not have been the most pleasant of subjects, but it worked. I was focused on something besides Nina and picturing her writhe and moan while I pleasured her body and made her feel things she had never felt before; gave her something to remember, something to gauge every future relationship on. A permanent expectation from every lover she would ever encounter because she doesn't just deserve better – she deserves the best.

"Where the hell did you go?" Colton asks, snapping his fingers in front of my face. "Oh shit, tell me you wrapped. I was joking."

I rise from my chair – ignoring his inquiries – and I square my eyes on the blonde sitting at the bar who's been shooting me come-hither looks and sultry smiles since I sat down. I'll confess, even in the midst of conflict, I don't miss a thing if it means I get laid in the end. I'm observant that way.

"I see a little slice of heaven over there that I think I'm going to…" I turn and smile, bobbing my eyebrows, "…take a bite out of. You okay getting your own taxi, or shall I see if she has a friend?"

He rolls his eyes. "I'm good. Think you might fix this one breakfast?"

"Bite your tongue." I scowl. "Breakfast is a menu item in a restaurant. And my sausage will never be found in a woman's kitchen the morning after."

And Sebastian Chambers is back to pumpin' and jumpin'… like his ass is on fire. Just like always. I don't leave them crying; I leave them wanting more. But more is the one thing they'll never get, the one thing I'll never give…because I don't have it to offer. There is only so much of me to go around and more is not on the menu.

The sheets are askew, the bed looks like it's hosted a small frat party, and she breathes heavily after her third orgasm. It reminds me of a dog I had when I was a kid. Her name was 'Sammy'. And when a woman reminds you of your childhood pet, well – let's just say the party's over.

I swing my legs over the side of the bed and collect the tied-off condoms from the trash can at the side of it. They're not evidence; they're a liability.

"Stay," she whines, reaching out for my arm and squeezing my bicep. "I promise you a morning wake-up call like you've never had. If you're a good boy, I'll fix you breakfast."

That's a boner killer right there.

Heading for the bathroom, clothes and used condoms in my hand, I reply the same as always, "I don't do breakfast."

Once in the bathroom, I pull the baggie out of my jeans pocket, drop the used condoms in it and stuff it back in the pocket. I wash my hands and get dressed.

Paranoid? No. Damn cautious? Damn right I am. Nothing like a turkey baster and creativity to nail a man to eighteen years of child support.

I open the bathroom door and see her on her knees, buck naked, in the middle of the bed, waiting for me to return. Shit! I should have waited for her to fall asleep and slipped out the door as usual. My skin is itchy, my nerves are on edge. My toes are curling inside my shoes.

"Maybe next time, you can stay all night?" she asks, her bottom lip puffed in a sultry pout. "How about next weekend?"

I arch a brow and dip my chin. "I made it clear, I'm up for a *good* time, not a *next* time. Good night, Sammy."

She grabs a pillow and throws it right before I close the bedroom door and screams, "It's Tammy!"

I knew that...sort of. Damn, I miss that dog.

Chapter 10

A Little Something Can't Hurt

Standing at the jewelry counter, I take in the necklaces, bracelets, watches, and rings. I've been up and down the aisle of display cases five times now, determined to find the proper gift to send to Nina for Christmas. I'm sending it to a friend of mine to hand deliver to the café. No sender's name attached, no identifying factors – just a gift for Nina. I contacted a friend of mine in Paris, called in a favor, and she'll make sure it gets done. Two weeks until Christmas and I need to get this gift sent overseas and delivered on time.

Yeah, yeah, you're wondering how Sebastian Chambers can have a female *friend*. She's gay, alright? That's how I can have a female friend. Feel better? She's an art student who's studying abroad. Had it been a guy, I'd be screwed. No way was I sending a guy in Nina's direction. And Serah had better not try to sway Nina into "experimenting" with anything. She's been warned.

Diamonds: Chocolate, canary, pink, blue. Who the hell knew diamonds came in different colors?

Pearls: Blue, pink, brown, white.

Gold, platinum, white gold, silver.

Watches: Big face, bold face, slim band, large band, smart watches. Would she want a smart watch?

Then I see them. Teardrop diamonds…necklace and earrings. Perfect. Just like the tears I saw roll down her cheeks that night on the beach. Should I get just the earrings? Yes. Two tears, two earrings. Makes sense, doesn't it? Maybe I'll get the matching set and save the necklace for my next visit. It's only five grand… pennies to me.

What the hell am I doing? I turn for the exit and storm out of the store. I've never bought a gift for a woman – other than my own mother – and let's face it, we all do that. I end up down the street about a block away and hesitate – pacing for a few moments – before I walk back to the jewelry store.

"May I help you?" the heavily perfumed, helmet-haired, middle-aged woman asks.

I point to the set displayed in the case. "That, that right there."

She raises her eyebrows. "What about it?"

"I want it."

She snorts and tries to hide an eye roll. "You need to fill out a credit application."

I realize I'm dressed in dark jeans, a Henley, and boots. My coat is nice – definitely nothing sloppy – but no doubt my attire falls short of the usual three-piece suits she deals with. However, people should not be judged by the clothes they wear, nor should a store clerk ever make someone feel less than because of it. I'll be wearing those suits five days a week for a good part of the rest of my life pretty soon, but I also know the value of comfort. I'll wear sweats when I damn well please and the last time I checked, my money spends the same in suits or sweats. Hell, my money spends pretty damn well when I'm buck naked. Just ask the pizza delivery guy.

I scowl, then fold my arms over my chest. "Are you the owner?"

She blushes as she draws a deep shaky breath and stutters, "Uh, no. I-I'm not."

I glance down to the end of the counter and see another salesperson finishing with a customer. "Excuse me," I call out to the younger, much prettier associate.

She walks towards us, smiling. "Yes, may I help you?"

Pointing to the same set I had moments ago, I say, "That right there. I'd like to make a purchase."

"Oh," she says brightly, pulling out her key to unlock the case. "That's one of my favorites, too." She unlocks the case and pulls out the necklace and earrings and sets them on the top of the counter. Turning to her coworker she asks, "Did you have trouble getting the case open?"

I reach into my back pocket, pull out my wallet and drop the black Amex onto the counter. "No, she was having trouble pulling the stick out of her ass."

* * *

By the time I leave the store, I'm carrying a bag with the diamonds for Nina, sapphires for my mom, a smart watch for Kinzie – the clerk deserved sales – and a new watch for my dad. I also bagged an evening with the sales associate. Drinks and sex at her place. Seems we both have a penchant for letting off steam. No strings, no repeats. And I'll make it my goal to be sure she's on Santa's naughty list. The only wrapped gift I'll be bringing is my dick.

* * *

Ah, Christmas at the country club. Men in tuxes, downing drinks as fast as they can be poured, comparing dick size by way of wallet thickness and stock portfolios. Women in gowns, licking those last-minute injection sites every thirty seconds to ensure their lips are still plumped, patting the styled updos on their heads as if they were attached pets, push-ups bras that leave their tits halfway between their shoulders and their chins. And those are the mothers of the wannabe future brides of America! The younger versions have no subtlety whatsoever. It's hard to discern cleavage from ass crack because their tits have been altered to a humungous size and the necklines on their dresses are cut so low. I'd bet there isn't a broom or coat closet in the place that isn't being utilized for fornication at this very moment. Even my own mother knows better than to try and pair me with the bimbos of the country club brand. Probably because she knows they've been branded by every dick in the county.

My parents, on the other hand, are of the small portion of dignified people who attend on behalf of charity. My dad wears the tux, and my mom wears the gown, but they present as classy, genuine people…because they are.

I won't speak for Colton's parents…because they aren't. I watch Mrs. Kinkaid work the room in her usual manner: elegant, poised, charming – the ultimate socialite. A little too perfect, a little too perky, a little too…much; as always. Mr. Kinkaid wears his usual façade of good dad, excellent businessman, stable character.

"What the hell are we doing here?" I ask Colton, tipping back my third whiskey of the evening.

He smirks, glancing around the room. "Charity."

"Hope you're feeling really charitable about now," I tell him, nodding toward the approaching the women. "Incoming. Looks like mommy has another prospect for you." I slap his shoulder before I make my usual fast escape. "Bro, I wouldn't bag that if I knew my dick was going to fall off tomorrow. I'm gonna go tell mom and dad goodnight and call for a driver. Make it fast and meet me in the car."

My laughter is not hidden on my way across the room as I hear Mrs. Kinkaid call out, "Colton, I have someone I'd like you to meet." I glance back over my shoulder and as God is my witness, I see steam coming from Colt's ears as he tolerates once again his mother's attempts at binding him in the ties of holy matrimony.

Just get it over with, Colt.

The car will be waiting.

The bar will be open.

There will be women – willing and wanting – by the time

we get there.

Five minutes and this nightmare will be over.

You can have a brunette…I'll take a redhead or a blonde.

'Tis the season…ho, ho, ho. Or is that ho, ho, hoes?

Chapter 11

"All Good Things Must Come to An End"

If it weren't for my parents I would have skipped this ceremony entirely. Suffering through high school and college graduation ceremonies was enough. The speeches, congratulations, awards, guest speakers, blah, blah, blah. The way I see it, this is five hours of my life I will never get back – five long, unbearable, excruciating hours.

We celebrated last night plenty. Technically, last night and this morning, until about three o'clock. And my eyeballs are on fire. The more I blink, the more they burn. The more they burn, the more they tear up. Worse than that, somebody's going to think I'm getting emotional when the truth is all I want is to get out of this gown, throw this damn cap somewhere into oblivion never to be found again, and cure this hangover with a few more drinks. The cap on my head feels like it weighs a ton and my temples pound. I shouldn't bitch about it; it's self-inflicted.

Just give me my damn diploma already.

Two days from now, my ass will be planted on a tropical beach, drink in hand, eyes on an endless stream of bikini-clad women; my dick deciding which one it'll be sliding into that evening. Did I say one? Correction: one at a time.

For one solid month after that I will be studying for the bar exam and then passing with flying colors. Then, and only then will I take a week in Europe. Well, after Grayson Kibbey's biggest mistake of his life. I'll believe it when I see it. Kinzie in white and Grayson in solid gray. *Fifty shades, maybe. Solid? Don't make me laugh.* Oxymorons. Take away the oxy and it's perfection. Two morons taking the leap into the depths of hell that awaits…eventual statistics.

I, Grayson, take thee….
Kibbey, Kibbey, Kibbey, where did we fail you?

* * *

"You ready for this?" Grayson asks, his satchel bag slung over his shoulder, keys in his hand. He's sweating bullets, caffeine-loaded, and looks like he's ready to puke up the breakfast he wolfed down not thirty minutes ago.

I grasp his shoulders tightly and hold him still. "Kibbey, I'm only going to tell you this once. You don't pass this bar exam and I will throw you into the Hudson wearing cement shoes."

His jaw hangs open, spit pools in the corner of his mouth. "You don't mean that. You know I can always take it again."

I slap his cheek gently – his open mouth making a hollow sound that reverberates throughout the kitchen – and narrow my eyes. "Bad ass men pass the bar exam the first time. You've got this."

"You know we don't have to take the exam to practice in Vermont," he stammers. "Even if I don't pass, I can still practice after I intern… Damnit!" He rubs the side of his head that I just smacked.

"We just spent three years in law school after spending four years busting our asses in college." I scowl, stepping closer and getting in his face. "If you think for one minute I'm going to spend more time working as a flunky for some law office in order to open my own practice, you're out of your fucking mind. Pull your head out of your ass, remember our goals, and go take the fucking exam."

He gets a sheepish grin, and I hear him choke back a laugh. "You know if you say fuck in front of a judge he's probably going to hold you in contempt."

I nod sharply. "I know. I have my own profanity prevention cure."

"What's that?"

"Picture my mother," I mutter as I turn away, my head hung low.

"What?" he asks, his voice light. "I missed that."

"Picture my mother," I grit through a clenched jaw. "Happy, asshole?"

He bursts in laughter mixed with a touch of smugness, because it's Kibbey, and he can't help himself. "Still tasting that soap, aren't you?"

"Let's go, smartass." I snatch my bag by the front door and turn the handle.

"Fresh and clean as a whistle," he imitates the accent from the old Irish Spring commercials and blows a wolf whistle. "Didn't taste as good as it smelled, did it?"

I turn to face him and smile slyly. "Ask Amanda Taylor. She thought it tasted pretty damn good."

He rolls his eyes and laughs. "Unbelievable. You had them kissing you back then?"

I smirk, arching a brow. "Kibbey, it wasn't my mouth she was tasting."

* * *

Bimini Should Rhyme with Bikini

"I really did need this," Colt says, tipping his head up towards the sun, relaxed in the lounge chair he occupies. "Thanks for talking me into it. Two weeks before I start classes again but I'm getting there."

"You can do this. The nameplate is already engraved." I swipe my hand through the air. "Colton B. Kinkaid, Esq. Had them done at the same time. We're on our way, Colt."

We bump fists and take another swallow of our drinks. I look at the scar that runs from his shoulder down his chest as he lies back on his lounger. He's come a long way in the last two years; finishing two years' worth of school in that time while needing six months to miraculously heal from an accident much better than predicted, gained back all of his faculties. He's always been a genius, finishing top of the class, star quarterback.

I don't envy the guy one bit – I admire the shit out of him.

And yet, I feel sorry for him. I would never tell him that though. He lost the love of his life and I saw how it broke him. I believe it pushed him to heal from the injuries – the anger he harbored deep inside – but he's never been the same since. He lost his sense of humor, the easygoing personality he always had. The soft side of Colt is gone. He's guarded, hard. He looks at women the way I do: a good time, a one-off. The Colton Kinkaid I knew all my life is gone, replaced with a replica of me. And this is not a good thing.

I look at the scar one more time. I know Jana Cooper isn't

responsible for the scar that runs from his shoulder to his chest. That one is all on Eaton Gunde. No, she's responsible for the invisible one that runs down the middle of his heart; the one that ripped it apart, the one the doctors couldn't fix. Apparently the one we can't either.

"I can't believe Kibbey passed up his last opportunity to join us for a tropical vacation."

Colt chuckles. "Sebastian, the man is going to be joined in wedded bliss in two weeks whether you like it or not. I hate to inform you, but the bromance is over."

"You really think it'll last?" I ask, the sour taste in my mouth increasing.

"Grayson's had a thing for Kinzie since the day he met her in the…" his voice trails off.

The burger joint where she sat with Jana the weekend Colt took Jana's virginity. Nobody knew it…Gray's secret crush. Just another reminder.

Two scantily clad ladies make their way down the beach, the tiny triangles of their bikini tops barely covering their nipples, the bottoms barely covering their asses. I drop my shades from the bridge of my nose, admiring the view before me.

"You want the pink or the yellow?" I ask Colt, seeing the women smile at us and wave.

He stretches his arms above him and yawns, laying back in his lounger. "Right now I want the blue…of the sky. Not looking to take a dip. They're all yours."

Maybe he's not a replica of me after all. I'll screw anything to keep Nina off my mind…to get her out of my system. Colt gets one little reminder of Jana, and his system shuts down. How can one woman hold so much power over him?

"Hmmm…" I shoot him an impish grin. "This could be fun. Haven't done doubles in a while."

He groans, "Just be sure to double wrap." He drops his shades and looks up, a wry smile spread on his face. "Shower before dinner or you're eating alone. Only looking to smell what *I'm* eating, thank you."

* * *

The bar exam is passed! For both Kibbey and me. I had no doubts, but seeing genuine proof brings relief I didn't think possible. The last step to achieving end results. The breaths I take feel like they're reaching the full depths of my lungs. I hadn't realized how shallow they had been prior to this. It's amazing how one doesn't always know just how much stress they're under until it's relieved. The difference between symptomatic treatment and a cure. Drinking and sex are symptomatic treatment; test scores are the cure.

Another One Bites the Dust

Grayson stands with his hands folded in front of him, calm as a cucumber, smile on his face, glowing like a little girl. His eyes shine – I swear I see tears gather on his lower lids as Kinzie makes her way down the aisle on her father's arm. Her mother sits dabbing at her eyes with a fancy cloth handkerchief, *my baby's getting married.* Colt and I stand at his side: his best men.

I want to punch him in the arm, box his ears, drag him out of here kicking and screaming. He'd get over it, realize we knew what was best for him. Sweep him off to Vegas for a few days of sin and sex and the man won't know what hit him, or what he was thinking when he agreed to this.

Marriage leads to monogamy…and white picket fences… and those dreaded little urchins that lock you down to a lifetime of responsibility. Two years ago it was hard enough to get Kibbey to put underwear on under his sweats. Hell, it was hard enough to get him to wear underwear or clothes of any kind in the apartment. How in the hell is he going to learn to change a damn diaper?

"Man up, shut up, and do your job," Colt mumbles low in my ear. "If you screw this up, I swear to God I will spread word you have an incurable social disease that you picked up in the tropics."

I flash him a glare that would normally make a man wilt in his shoes, but it only makes him smile nonchalantly, shrug and whisper, "More for me."

I mouth, "Asshole."

* * *

"I now pronounce you husband and wife," the preacher announces. "You may kiss…"

"My ass," I mutter before Colt elbows me in the ribs.

"You almost made it," Colt says with a laugh as the church roars with cheers at the couple's first wedded kiss.

"See that?" I tilt my head towards Gray and Kinzie as they share an extra kiss. "The beginning of the end."

Colt shakes his head and chides, "Forever the cynic."

"Hey, I'm doing my part to make for a lasting relationship. I chose the perfect wedding gift."

He eyes me skeptically. "What?"

"A lifetime supply of aprons and dishtowels…" I smirk. "…all embroidered 'submissive'. I didn't want Gray to get his suits soiled."

"And for Kinzie?" he asks, brow arched.

"What else?" I shrug. "A nut cup with a handle so she can drag him around by the balls."

Chapter 12

It was inevitable

The minute my ass hits the seat on the plane, my body relaxes. I've waited over a year to do this. It's two months later than my usual trip due to the bar exam, Gray's wedding, and the vacation I determined was needed to get Colt out of his head. I owed it to him. What is normally a late spring trip has turned into August.

What's worse is this year I'm only staying for one week versus two. It was an internal war for months. Nina is my refuge, my *untouchable* refuge. I'd never make it two weeks again. She's older now, not *as* untouchable, but still a vow to myself to never ruin what we have. This fourth trip could be my breaking point if I stay too long. Seven days…seven short days.

Once again, I've convinced myself this trip is so I can see how she is, check on her, reassure myself she's okay. I know better though. Nina is my conscience cleanse. My yearly self-inflicted punishment. I'm not so unrealistic as to know this won't end…I'm just not ready yet. I'm not what she needs – she's what I need.

My flight lands early morning this time. I managed to get some sleep on the flight; not much, but enough. There were no law books to study, no podcasts I felt obligated to listen to; nothing but the thoughts swimming in my head and eventually those thoughts allowed me to drift into slumber – restless as it was.

Checking into my hotel is uneventful, my bags delivered to my room by concierge, a welcome basket and champagne sitting on the table.

I grab a shower, change clothes and have breakfast. In the afternoon, I head down to the familiar neighborhood where I know I will find her at the café waiting tables, serving patrons.

I stand in my usual spot across the street, hidden in the shadows at the corner of the old brick building, waiting to spot her. The patio is full, every table occupied. I smile to myself as I wait for her to appear. The servers pass each other as they make their way from table to table and back to the kitchen to replenish the orders. No Nina.

A full hour of watching and waiting passes. The patio tables empty of one group after another only to be filled by the next. I check my watch from time to time as my worry grows. She's not here. Maybe it's her day off, I try to reassure myself. I watch for another half hour. I see a short-haired brunette wait a table and I eye her closely. It's not her. She didn't cut her hair. I spin around on occasion, checking the sidewalks behind me. She's not here.

I pull my phone from my pocket and find Serah in my directory.

"Sebastian!" she answers cheerily. "To what do I owe the pleasure?"

"Hey, Serah," I reply. "I need to ask you a question."

"Hey, Serah," she mimics cheekily. "It's been so long. How are you? How's school? Got any hot girlfriends who aren't gay that you can hook me up with?"

I roll my eyes as I pinch the bridge of my nose. She's right. I should have asked how she was first. We don't talk often, and it was a lousy way to open a conversation.

"I'm sorry," I say sincerely, then blow out a breath. "How are you sweet cheeks?"

She laughs. "I'm good. What's up Scout? Still rescuing

damsels in distress?"

I chuckle at her nickname for me. I met Serah my junior year of college when she was struggling with an asshole in a bar one night. He couldn't take no for an answer and I simply taught him what it meant. How hard can it be? The shortest word in the English language…sort of, and the first word you teach a kid if you want them to be safe. He left black and blue and she left…my friend.

The nickname Scout came from my helping her find an art school to attend as well as a mentor who would help her soar to the heights of her talent – which happen to be profound – and we have remained friends for the last five years. She's like a little sister to me.

"The diamonds I sent at Christmas," I remind her. "Did you make sure they got to the correct recipient?"

"Of course I did," she reassures me. "I stood right there as she opened your gift. I told you that when I called."

"And you didn't tell her who they were from?"

"Sebastian," she chides. "I followed your instructions exactly as you directed. Is there a problem?"

"No," I grunt, my hopes falling with every second. "No problem. I was just checking."

"Hey," she hums soothingly. "Talk to me. What's going on?"

"She's not here, Serah," I tell her, my voice filled with resignation. "She's not at the café.

Her voice lights with excitement. "You're in Paris? You're at the café?"

"Yeah," I grumble.

"Stay there," she orders. "I'll meet you in fifteen minutes."

Exactly eighteen minutes later I see Serah standing outside the black wrought iron fencing that surrounds the café, scoping the patio for me. I call her name as I cross the street to meet her.

"Sebastian!" she calls out as she greets me with hug, jumping into my arms, clinging tightly to my neck and kissing my cheek. "My hero."

I chuckle as I set her back on her feet. "Nobody's hero, Serah. Just an everyday chump."

She pats me on the cheek. "Well, chump, let's go find your girl."

Serah is definitely more fluent in French than I am. I can speak it, yes, but I'm rusty as hell. In the process of speaking with every employee here, we find it's a dead-end street.

Nina is gone.

She quit last month, two weeks ago. I missed her by two weeks.

Nina Lafon is no longer here.

"You have her address," Serah says. "Let's try it. You've got nothing to lose, Sebastian. I'll go to the door. You wait in the car."

We visit the 17th arrondissement. The complex is enormous, but I remember the building where I delivered Nina multiple times. I lean against the car watching as Serah makes her way into the building and I wait outside…patiently, for what seems like a lifetime.

I then watch as Serah exits the building, shoulders not as straight as when she entered, eyes not meeting mine until she arrives at my side. Her lips twist and she looks to the sky before she finally breaks the news.

"The family moved two weeks ago," she says.

"What? Where did they go?" I can feel that damn organ between my throat and my belly swell as acid rises in my throat. I swallow hard. "Where did they go, Serah?"

She shakes her head and whispers, "The new tenant doesn't know. I talked to a neighbor and they didn't have any answers either. I'm sorry, Sebastian." She shrugs. "The neighbor said Nina's been different lately, sad. Her parents took different jobs and took Nina with them because of a man they didn't want her with. They said she was starting at some cooking school, but they have no idea where."

I feel like the wind has been knocked out of me. What was I supposed to expect? I left her behind every year to go back to my own life, leaving her here to live hers. Apparently, that's exactly what happened. The very thought of her being with another man stirs something inside of me I never thought I would feel… *jealousy.* The angry green monster that lives within all of us.

Serah slides her arm through mine. "I'm sorry, Scout. Don't leave. Spend this time with me. We haven't seen each other in forever." She leans her head on my shoulder and looks up from under long, thick mascara-coated lashes; batting them flirtatiously, and smiles brightly as she proffers, "Drink each other under the table and commiserate in a purely platonic friends with no benefits way?" She waves her hand at my crotch. "Because, you know…I don't do dick."

I chuckle softly. Serah is hilarious and I know she's trying so hard to soothe what she thinks is a broken heart. Little does she know; I don't have one. Whatever that chunk in my chest is just went into lockdown. But I do care…about her, my friends, my family. I throw my arm over her shoulder and kiss the top of her head.

"You got it, kiddo."

So I spend the next week with Serah and her friends, in a drunken stupor, alone in my hotel room each night with the exception of one brunette – the night I was just sober enough to double wrap. I give the woman a couple orgasms and take a couple for myself. Guilt so overwhelming the next morning I couldn't look in the mirror.

What was her name? Doesn't matter. It wasn't her face I was seeing anyway.

And then I go home.

Without seeing Nina.

Without hearing my name whispered the only way she can.

Without seeing those eyes filled with hope, eyes that gave me hope. Eyes that proved to me I have a heart.

Correction: Had a heart.

What was I thinking? I was never good enough for her.

Selfish bastards don't win…we function.

Chapter 13

"What happens in this office stays in this office"

"Absolutely not," I snap harshly without hesitation. My jaw tics as I square my eyes on Grayson and he winces. He knew what the answer would be before he posed the question. "She will not work in this office. And if she finds work with the DA's office, we're going to have a real conflict here, Gray. Tell her to get her little ass into a comfy corporate office and stay the hell away from what we're doing."

"That's taking it too far, Chambers," he screams. "You can't tell my wife where she can work!"

Little does he know, a conflict of interest of this proportion most certainly does put me in a position to make decisions, be it for Kinzie or for him. We are a partnership of three. We have our own paralegals, secretaries, interns, etc. I don't need his *wifey* in our office. I'm not going to deal with marital spats, fucking in his office when it's ovulation time, or installing a daycare in the building when she decides she doesn't want to be separated from the little rug rat; not to mention pulling a tit out at feeding time. I also don't need them discussing cases outside the office i.e. at home in the bedroom.

"No," I reply, my eyes narrowed. "But I can tell her one place she won't work. And we certainly can take a vote and decide whether or not we're willing to compromise our cases in lieu of keeping a partnership with you in order to keep your vows intact. Deal. With. Your. Wife."

"You're a real prick, you know that?" he huffs, his hands clenched at his sides so tight his knuckles turn white. "What would be the problem with Kinz working for the same side?"

"Gentlemen," Colt interjects. "Calm down." He sighs heavily and looks to Gray. "We did agree on a three-man partnership, Grayson."

"But…" Grayson protests.

Colt raises his hand. "Hear me out. The three of us have a connection that you don't see anywhere else. Gray, I know you love Kinz. Good on you, congrats. Whatever. And she's a good paralegal. But an agreement is an agreement. No family in the office. I'm solid with Chambers on that one. As far as working for the DA? I think she'd be too close to the cases in our office. You guys would be living and breathing work together. Not healthy. You sure this isn't about Kinzie wanting the excitement you have?"

His shoulders sag as his cheeks puff before he heaves a sigh and rolls his eyes. "I don't know what it is. She's bored. She thinks we might have a better connection if we work on the same type of cases."

I lean forward in my chair, my elbows on my desk, and smirk. "You want a better connection? Throw one of her legs over your shoulder. Ride her doggy style. I don't care. She's not working in this office." I point to the door. "Now, out. I have work to do."

Grayson glowers as he stands at the door. "You're a real asshole."

Shrugging casually, I answer, "Never said I wasn't."

He slams the door on his way out, making the walls rumble.

"You need to fix this," Colt warns.

I pick up a folder and toss it back down on my desk, resigned. "I know. I will."

"What's going on with you?" he asks, his brow creased. I

hear the concern in his voice. "You've been on edge for months. Got a case that's bugging you?"

Yeah, I've got a case. She's somewhere in France, I think, and I missed her by two weeks. Two fucking weeks! Ten months ago and I still can't get her out of my head. She left...she left me. I'm bitter, grouchy, empty. That's what I am...empty. And lonely. I haven't seen her in nearly two years and yet, I remember exactly what she feels like, sounds like, tastes like.

"Must be a helluva case," Colt says, snapping me out of my thoughts. He stands and walks to the door, turning the knob but stops before he opens it. "If you decide you want some help, let me know."

"Will do."

"Sebastian," he hesitates. "Whatever it is, don't take it out on Gray. He's the good guy. I can guarantee you, it's not his fault."

Colton has been active in the practice for five months. He keeps us balanced, even, aimed. He's a king in the courtroom; has yet to lose a case. None of us have. His empty stare I notice every once in a while when I pass his office though; it's like he's reverting. I'm finally starting to understand his sense of loss. I swore I would never let a woman have that kind of control over my thoughts and yet......

Colton hasn't taken a woman home in months. He leaves the bar alone every time while I can't seem to leave without a guarantee of a couple hours of entertainment. We live in the same building – penthouses – two floors between us.

My hand was raised to knock on his door one night; the intention to slam back a drink or two before calling it a day. Sad, sappy music rang out from the inside and I pulled my hand back like the door was hot coals. My idea of sad music is a country tune that belts lyrics about the wife runnin' off with the truck and the dog and leavin' the kids behind, but this was music that our parents probably listened to. A song about a woman named *"Aubrey"* and *"she had been mine for a day"*. Worst part? I didn't walk away. No, I sat down in the hallway and listened, feeling the pit in my stomach while picturing Nina. Best part? At least Colt wasn't crooning along with it.

Saddest part of all? I searched for that song. Found it as well as the entire soundtrack which now is part of my collection. A collection I have a tendency to listen to far too often. *"Anthology of Bread"*. I'll deny it until the day I die. Total lie. I will die before I ever admit it.

Now I have Grayson to deal with, all because of a woman – his wife. The woman he loves. It's said, "You can't live with them, can't live without them". I'm here to tell you there's truth in that statement; Colt and I seem to be simply existing.

* * *

I stand in Gray's doorway, head down, ashamed of the way I attacked him earlier. Colt's right; it's not his fault. "You want to get a drink before you go home?"

"Nope," he answers, popping the "P" for emphasis.

"I'm sorry," I grumble. "For being an asshole."

He snorts, throwing a pen on his desk. "You ought to have that written on a T-shirt."

"I do. It's an altered version," I tell him. "Mine reads, 'Asshole, no apologies'. I'm making an exception in your case."

He laughs, finally, and drops his head in his hands. "God, Chambers. What's going on with us?"

Walking over to his desk, I place my hands on his shoulders and lean down to whisper in his ear, "Lovers' quarrel. If you won't tell, I won't tell. Let's go get a drink, honey. Kiss and make up?"

"Blow job?" he quips, matching my smartassery.

"Open wide sweetheart, I knew you were missing my dick," I whisper softly and lightly blow in his ear.

"You asshole!" he growls, brushing his ear with his hand like it's contaminated.

I stand tall and walk to the door. I turn and wink. "No apologies."

He grabs his jacket from the hook, punches my arm, and we walk down the hall to fetch Colton. "You okay, Seb? You seem to have something on your mind lately."

"Nothing a little extra sleep won't take care of," I reply.

"Phew," he says as he shakes his head. "I figured you either weren't getting laid or were waiting for paternity results."

I shoot him a side-eye with a wry smile. "Me – not get laid. Funny man, Kibbey. I'll be eighty and still getting laid on the reg."

Colton sticks his head out the door of his office. "Was that on the reg or the rug?"

In unison Kibbey and I grin and say, "Both."

Gray stayed for one drink and had Kinzie pick him up. Colton stayed for dinner as well as a couple more drinks. I stayed even longer for…more. Colt called for a ride, I called for a ride for two. And so the story goes…

I was home by midnight; physically sated. Ready for bed half an hour later; tired. In bed at two o'clock; wide awake, staring at the ceiling. Empty, lonely, and wanting…what I can't have.

I'm not going to Europe this summer. What's the point? She's not there anymore, at least not where I can find her. I've thought about hiring someone to search for her – after I'd done my own search through every branch of social media without success – just to check on her, see how she is, make sure she's okay.

Right. Keep telling yourself that, Chambers.

'A man her parents didn't want her with'. The words Serah recited play on repeat through my mind. The words the neighbor used. Had he hurt her? Had she fallen in love? Did she let him do to her the things I had done? Did she compare him to me? I hope so. Because let's face it, if she did she was seeing my face. Just like I see hers…all the damn time.

Since I'm not going to Europe, I may as well stay here and work. I could take a vacation anywhere, but at best it would only give me more time to think. I'll get past this; I know I will.

This past year I've become angrier, harder, colder – which makes me a ruthless prosecutor – gives me an edge in the courtroom, relentless in my pursuit of happiness and justice for those who have lost, suffered, and persevered through damages and pain caused by others.

Chapter 14

"We're checking for brain damage"

It's seven o'clock when I check the screen on my phone as it buzzes. "Hey, Colt. What's up?"

"Just leaving the 'rents," he says. "You want to get a drink? I haven't had dinner. I can meet you at Zimbarra's in half an hour."

My laughter cannot be restrained as I respond, "Just leaving the 'rents and you need a drink? Surprise. Are we walking?"

"Well, yeah. It's five minutes from home, dipshit."

"And I'm two floors down from you. Knock on your way down and I'll walk with you…" I hesitate for emphasis before I finish, "…dipshit."

I wait for him in the hallway outside his door as I had nothing to do downstairs and quite frankly, I was getting restless.

He exits the elevator and sees me standing by his door. He eyes me skeptically and sighs. "Tell me you weren't banging 20B before I got here."

"Nah, she wasn't home." I wasn't banging anybody; he should know better. I take my time, never rush a good thing. I haven't seen the inside of a bathroom for a quickie since college. I have acquired manners and patience in advancing years.

He arches a brow. "Get restless waiting for me?"

"Just making sure you didn't forget."

He rolls his eyes and slips his key in the lock. "I called you, dumbass."

"I called you dumbass first," I remind him, laughing. "I think it was freshman year when you told Zanie you would show her your winky." *I said I've acquired manners and patience. I didn't say I've matured.*

"Get in here," he growls. "You could have just let yourself in. Let me drop my briefcase and get out of this monkey suit."

It's true, I could have let myself in. We both have keys to each other's place with an open-door policy at any given time.

* * *

Sitting at a hi-top table we order our first round of drinks and dinner. From Colton's somber expression, something tells me we'll be having more than one drink tonight.

"So," I start. "Stopped at mom and dad's. Special occasion or self-inflicted punishment tonight?"

He hesitates, working the knots out of his neck with a bit of twisting and turning before answering, "Needed a reminder."

I sigh, thinking the last thing he needs is a reminder of his childhood, but I know that's not what this is about. "Reminder of what?"

He proceeds to tell me about his mother's antics to once again set him up with another prospect from a rich family while we eat our dinner. We laugh, swap a few jokes regarding wet spots on sofas and so forth. And then he drops the bomb. He needed the reminder of why he hates…Jana.

"Okay, Colt. Tell me what's going on."

The dazed look I see once in a while, the pain in his eyes when he stares into space returns before he squeezes them closed. "She's back, Seb. I saw her."

There's only one person he uses that tone of voice for – his nightmare.

Jana Cooper is back.

And she has a kid.

His kid – supposedly. Not that she's told him that; he's convinced of it. Because of the physical similarities. A living, breathing urchin that sucks the life out of you and makes you go all…stupid!

"You want the kid?" I ask, searching his face, desperate to hear him stand his ground and fight for his dignity.

I see the pain, the struggle. I hear the desperation from so long ago once again as he whispers, "I want them both."

See! Stupid!

It's official: My best friend has lost his fucking mind.

No, the doctors missed something. Brain damage, personality disorder caused by the accident…because the man I am looking at is not the Colton Kinkaid I know. His eyes are softer, he's sentimental, he's…he's…falling down the rabbit hole again.

"Un…fucking…believable," I growl, standing from my seat, tossing a tip on the table. "Let's go. I've got an early morning and I'm too tired for this shit tonight. We'll ponder the thoughts of Colton Kinkaid's head that's up his ass tomorrow. I swear to God you suffered brain damage. I don't care what the doctors say."

I never did like that woman

I knew Mrs. Kinkaid was a lousy parent, but never in my wildest dreams did I believe someone could be so evil. To be able to watch her son hurt the way Colton did, wreak the havoc she did, see the devastation she had caused and walk amongst the ruins as if there were none. Ever look up the definition of sociopath? It's Mrs. Kinkaid. She kept a lie alive for five years and fed on it as if it were manna from heaven.

Welcome to hell, Mrs. Kinkaid.

My mother sees Colton as a second son. Colt was at my house more than he was his own as a kid. He was comfortable with my family. They were more than accommodating with him; movie nights, popcorn, never missed our little league ballgames or college football games and cheered us both on because his parents were always absent.

My mother was more than happy to present the pictures I sent her from Colton's phone to all the ladies at the country club luncheon. The son of Colton and his now fiancé Jana Cooper – the woman Mrs. Kinkaid had been lying about for the last five years. The woman she lied to five years ago when Colton was in the accident. The woman she gave a note to – supposedly from Colton – informing her that he had left for Stanford, wishing her well and telling her goodbye. A note that changed, and temporarily ruined, the lives of three people. All because Mrs. Kinkaid didn't deem Jana *an appropriate fit* for her social circle. Mrs. Kinkaid left in a hurry – blacklisted by her socialite circle – the new gossip subject for years to come.

Colt missed four years watching his son grow up. He missed five years with the love of his life. She didn't leave him after all. She believed he had left her.

Chapter 15

"Don't make me call you dumbass last"

They're doing it. My best friend is getting married to the love of his life. I've never seen Colt stand straighter, taller, prouder – never seen him so happy. He's finally got everything. His kid's pretty cute too. Feisty, smart, potty-trained. *Dodged a bullet on that one, Kinkaid.* Although dumping Cheerios in the toilet bowl for aiming could be fun. I hear people paint targets in the bowl too. Hey! I know. A picture of Mrs. K's face and I would piss on that daily. My housekeeper would be so happy with me, she'd be leaving me treats twice a week instead of the notes she currently does:

"If you sprinkle when you tinkle, be a sweetie and wipe the seatie," or *"My aim at the shooting range is better. Think about that for a moment."*

I smile to myself – the toilet bowl thoughts running through my head – as I sit and watch the crowded dance floor, the reception well underway. The wedding took place with one week of planning. Colt's grandfather worked his usual charm, aka power, to get the club to open the biggest room. The cake is perfection; three tiers of sugary goodness. I should know, I've already indulged in two slices. The liquor pours. I should also know; I've indulged in plenty of that as well.

The tux I wear isn't too stifling although naked is my preferred choice, but I can bear the burden for another couple hours. I scope the room, searching for a delectable piece of ass to take to the nearest hotel, or her place, when my best man duties are over. There's a pit in my stomach when dawning smatters my thoughts: my two best friends are now hitched. I'm the odd man out. But that just means more for me, right?

I'm suddenly getting sick to my stomach. Is it my thoughts? The food? The fear of being the odd man out? I get a rush up my spine and my head feels dizzy. I take some long, slow, deep breaths. Is this a panic attack? I loosen my tie and unbutton my collar. *That's better.*

I glance around the room. People are moving just as they were moments ago but something's off; I can feel it. My senses go on high alert. The hair on my arms and neck stand on end, my fingers tingle and my heart starts to race. It's the wedding, the atmosphere, I tell myself. But there is only one trigger for these sensations, and it's impossible. I'm here and she's…God knows where. Then my nostrils are filled with – her scent. It's her own; homemade from herbs and flowers that she designed herself. There is no other scent like it. It's all Nina.

I stand and turn slowly. I know exactly where she is, I can feel her now. She stands at a table, talking to a couple who look up at her and smile. I wait patiently for her to turn around, my heart pounding my chest. When she turns she doesn't see me, so I wait for her to get closer before I call her name.

"Nina?" Even through my shock and awe at seeing her standing before me, her name leaves my lips numb. I've whispered it so many times in the dark, like a prayer that went unanswered. I swore to myself if I saw her again, I would tell her the truth.

Her eyes meet mine and her hand covers her heart. "Bast?"

I see the necklace I gave her before her fingers close around it. The earrings dangle below her earlobes and sparkle in the light. *She still wears them.*

"Wha…why…uh…when did you…" I'm suddenly speechless. I want to pull her into my arms and never let go. "It… it's good to see you," I stutter, reaching for her. "Wh…what are you doing here?"

She face falls as her eyes rim with tears. "*Ma grand-pe`re mourir.*" (Her grandfather died)

"I'm sorry," I whisper softly, pulling her into my arms, placing a kiss on the top of her head. "But, Nina, what are you doing here? Here at this place?"

She pulls back from my hug, a sudden burst of energy overcomes her as she explains excitedly, "*Ma cousin travail ici. I travail ici. Je suis rester ici.*" Her cousin works here, she works here, and apparently she plans on staying.

I'm confused. "Nina, your grand-pe`re lived in New York. Why are you here?"

"*Pour te trouver,*" she says as if I should know.

To find me. She came for me? My stomach roils and the heaviness in my chest makes it hard to breathe. What do I have to offer her? She is innocence personified, nothing's changed, I see it in her eyes. I'm used goods. Hell, I'm over-used goods. My sexual proclivities the last two years would probably have made Hugh Hefner blush. I have been literally trying to pump her out of my system – no pun intended. She deserves better.

"Nina," I sigh, the crack in my chest growing. "You need to go home."

She stares at me, incredulous. Her chin starts to tremble, tears building in her eyes. I can literally feel her heart breaking. She whispers softly, "*Tu es bien a` en quittant. Tu aller hom.*" You are good at leaving. You go home.

"Nina," I plead.

I've never felt the pain of a knife through my heart – metaphorically or otherwise – until now when she says, "*Je t`ai attendu, S`ebastien. Tu n`es jamais venu.*"

She waited for me and I never came. But I did come. She was gone.

She turns on her heel and walks away, her head hung low.

I stand and watch, my heart traipsing behind with every footstep that she takes.

I hear Colton's feigned wistful sarcasm beside me. "Another broken heart?"

Rubbing my temples with my middle finger and thumb, feeling the pressure from the headache coming on. "I am so fucked…"

He crinkles his nose. "She's a little young."

"Which is why I didn't *get* fucked."

"Her choice or yours?"

"Fuck you," I growl.

"Wow. Three fucks in a row." He laughs. "Must have been hers."

"It was mine," I grit through a clenched jaw. "I was not about to break through something so delicate."

Colton's shoulders rock in silent laughter.

"What's so funny asshole?"

"Sebastian Chambers has morals," he says, patting me on the shoulder. "Couldn't deflower the flower. Don't worry, your secret's safe with me. How old is she?"

Furrowing my brow, I calculate quickly in my head and rub chin my before I answer, "Must be twenty-one by now."

Shooting me a cocky grin and a cheek click; he winks. "Lucky you. You can dine her…and wine her."

"Piss off. Not my type."

The asshole reaches out and flicks my chin. "Yeah, that's why you have drool running out of the corner of your mouth."

"It's not like that." I sigh heavily, staring at the hallway she just walked down. "She's the kind of girl you take for walks on the beach, strolls in the park, have coffee on the patio with at a café." I shake my head, acquiescing. "She's the one you watch a sunset with, and then lie down in the grass and watch the stars come out after."

"Did you enjoy doing all of those things, Sebastian?"

I scoff and internally chastise myself at the mere thought of having someone as good as Nina to myself. "Doesn't matter. I'm the guy who's dipped his dick in more women than pretzels get dipped in cheese at football games. She deserves better."

"So, were you not the better guy when you were with her?"

"Colt." I run my hands through my hair in frustration and yank on it. "She deserves better!"

"She deserves to be loved, and so do you. I would say go wash the cheese off your dick, start fresh, and enjoy those sunsets and stars."

"Colt…"

He grabs my shoulders like only he can get away with. "Listen to me, dumbass. You are the best man I have ever known. I couldn't ask for a better friend and I've never forgotten what you did for me. That woman showed up here tonight for a reason. Be the man she deserves. And whether you believe it or not, you deserve the best. And if you think that's her, go get her."

I have no doubt she's the best. And I am a better man when I'm with her. But can I be the best?

Jana calls for Colton from across the room.

"That's my cue," he tells me. "Now go find her. Make things right."

"I'll try. Thanks, Colt."

"No problem," he says and then mutters, *cradle robber.*

"I heard that, asshole!"

He spins back around and snaps his fingers loudly. "Wait a minute…she's the reason you went back to Europe every year and the same reason you don't do brunettes, isn't she?"

I feel the heat in my cheeks and sigh. "Busted."

"Aww," he drawls, fighting a grin. "You were saving yourself. Your mom would be so proud. A fountain of youth could lead to a gaggle of grandbabies."

"Are you finished, jackass?" Although hearing him say it aloud doesn't make me run for the door like my ass is on fire. I could paint a target in a toilet bowl and teach my little guy how to aim for the bullseye. I could learn to play with Barbie dolls and how to braid hair.

"Think so," Colt says. I'm pretty sure he was referring to

being finished. I was too lost in my thoughts of fatherhood. "By the way," he says. "Word has it there is a Frenchman sitting outside in a pickup truck with a shotgun. Might want to lay low for a while."

I scowl. "You just don't give up, do you?"

His words take us back to a time neither one of us will ever forget. "My best friend told me years ago I wasn't allowed to. Glad I listened to him."

"Wish me luck?"

"You won't need it," he reassures me. "Call me if you need me."

"It's your wedding night! Don't think so."

"Call me in the morning."

"Hey, Colt?"

"Yeah?"

"Can I borrow Briggs tomorrow?"

He pauses. "Excuse me?"

"Nina loves puppies. I thought we could take him around to check on some…" I use air quotes "…barnyards," – indicating Briggs' mispronunciation of Bernard – as in dog.

He snorts loudly. "Are you kidding me?"

I lift a shoulder, shrugging sheepishly. "I want to take him on like a trial run, you know?"

"Sebastian," he huffs. "You test drive cars, not kids. You can't return them if they're dented or scratched."

Is he sure about that?

"Get over here for the garter toss," he says.

"I'm not that far gone!"

"You never were." He arches a brow. "And you're not that guy anymore. C'mon, Chambers!"

The ladies go through the bouquet toss and I watch from the sidelines. Ah, weddings. The only time women are so much more eager to catch a bunch of flowers than men are to catch a piece of lingerie. Men will pay good money any day of the week to watch a strip tease in a bar and hold that garter up like a trophy. But put them at a wedding and they treat it like a choke collar that's been dipped in dog shit.

At Grayson's wedding, I conveniently had to piss when the garter was thrown, as I always do. Seems wedding garters and I have something in common: a mutual disdain.

Tonight, however, out of obligation to the best friend I've ever had, I join the misfits on the floor and await my fate. I swear to God, Colton aims it at my chest and sure as shit, it lands dead center. For some odd reason, I hold it up like a trophy tonight instead of tossing it like a dreaded collar, and smile.

Colt points to the hallway and yells, "Go! I'll see you later."

"Wish me luck!" I yell back.

"You don't need it! There's a sunset coming, take a blanket!"

The smartass in me surfaces. "I'll keep her warm!"

"Don't be a dumbass!" he warns me.

"I called you dumbass first!" I retort.

"Don't make me call you dumbass last!" He raises his hand high in the air. "Give me that garter!"

I hold it up, twirling it on my finger, then drop it into my palm and study it for a moment. I can be her best…or die trying.

"Someday," I yell as I toss it back to Colton.

"I'll be there," he shouts.

"Counting on it." I wave before I make my way to the hall that holds the promise to my future.

Chapter 16

"I was two weeks late"

She's not a server, not a hostess, not a cook. No, Nina is the head fucking chef! Dinner is long over, and the kitchen is bustling with clean up duties. How did I not notice the white chef's coat she wore in the banquet room? Because I was too lost in Nina. Too busy noting the necklace and earrings she wore. Too busy getting lost in the eyes I've missed gazing into for the last two and a half years.

Standing off to the side of the entrance to the kitchen, I observe her in all her glory. So organized. She doesn't bark orders. She works right alongside the rest of the staff, moving them along like an assembly line. Wiping down counters, sanitizing everything before it goes back in the fridge. She speaks to them in perfect English, heavily frosted with her French accent.

She was testing me by speaking French. Yet, I understood every word perfectly. She thinks I abandoned her. She thinks I never came back. But I did, and she wasn't there. I missed her . . . by two weeks. And I had no idea where she had gone.

I know she knows I'm here. All she has to do is look up.

Look up and see me, Nina. I'm here. I'm sorry. So damn

sorry. Forgive me, please.

Finally.

Her eyes find their way to mine, and I see in them what I've missed so much since I left Paris the last time I saw her. I see home.

I mouth the words I've been longing to say for the past two years. "I love you."

As fast as her feet can carry her she's across the room and in my arms as I lift her off her feet. I had no idea just how empty I had been until this very moment. She fits perfectly, her body with mine, her soft with my hard. She fills every crack and crevice in my brokenness. I wasn't living without her; I was existing. It's no wonder I could easily say I didn't have a heart – I had left it with her.

"S`ebastien," she whispers in my ear. Nobody says it like Nina. I bury my face in the crook of her neck and breathe her in; the intoxicating scent taking me back in time to the last place I was truly happy and at peace. It wasn't so much a place though because it was her. It didn't matter where…as long as she was there.

"Nina," I whisper, closing my eyes and praying I don't wake up and find her gone like I so often have from my dreams.

The kitchen erupts in applause and cheers and I feel Nina's body gently shake in giggles. She pulls back just enough to look at me and smile. "They are happy for me."

I kiss her, like I've never kissed her before. I put every last emotion I have into it. She needs to know how much I've missed her, how much I need her, how much I love her.

"Watch a sunset with me?" I ask when the kiss is over, leaning my forehead on hers. I feel her nod against my forehead. "And then we'll watch the stars come out?"

She pulls back, her brow furrows. "And then?"

"And then I'll take you home with me." Her smile says all I need but the kiss she adds is confirmation I've given her the answer she wanted.

"Hey, cuz," a multicolor-haired woman with nose rings says as she approaches us. "So, this is the stud you've been pining over." She steps around us, blatantly assessing me from head-to-toe, tilting her head and nodding. "Not bad, not bad. I prefer blondes, but–" She pulls the tails up on my tux. "–nice ass. He'll do."

Nina giggles. "Roz!"

The woman shrugs at Nina and rolls her eyes. "Five years in the making and you in tears for the last two!" she shrieks, then turns to me with a fierceness in her eyes that makes me shrivel. "You ever hurt her again and I will hunt you down like a dog. Now get her out of here and make an honest woman out of her."

Nina shrugs off her chef's jacket and hands it to her cohort after introducing her as her cousin, Roz. We stop at her locker to get her purse and as we're on our way out the door…

"Chambers!" Grayson shouts. Shit! We should have gone out the back door, but the driver is out front. Evening is approaching and I would love to get Nina down by the lakeside before we miss the sunset. I've already hesitated so he knows I heard him. I could be a real ass and continue walking, but Nina heard him as well and has stopped walking entirely, anticipating my acknowledgement of my pain in the ass friend.

"Yes, Gray?" I say as I turn in his direction.

"You headed out already?" he asks, a knowing grin plastered on his cockblocking mug. Little does he know Nina wants out of here as much or more than I do. He nods towards the banquet room. "There's more celebration in there. We have to see the bride and groom off. Don't forget we have manny duties this week." He winks at Nina. "Good practice for us future daddies."

I'm gonna choke this asshole come Monday. Yes, Gray, I know we have *manny duties* this week. I'm taking on some tomorrow afternoon to look at "barnyards" because I opened my big mouth before thinking it through.

Colton and Jana are spending their honeymoon in New York while Jana's father has surgery for cancer treatment. Not exactly what one would call a honeymoon, but the rest of us are sharing care for their son while they're away. It also means Gray and I have no chance of time off work this next week because we will already be one short in the office with Colton gone. I have two overnights with little Briggs, at their home no less, and I have no idea what that leaves me with Nina. Uncle Tyler will be in New York as well so that leaves Gray, Grandpa Briggs and me as mannies.

"What are manny duties?" Nina asks, eyes curious.

Gray's eyes light as Nina speaks and he grins. "I like your accent," he says. "You'll have to pardon my friend's rudeness. Seems Sebastian has neglected to introduce us." He extends his hand. "I'm Grayson Kibbey, Seb's law partner. And you would be the lovely…"

Nina blushes but extends her hand. "Nina Lafon."

I place my arm around her shoulders, pull her close and kiss her temple. "My girlfriend," I announce. She smiles shyly and peeks up through dark, thick lashes. As I look at her, I realize she's so much more. "I love you."

"I love you, S`ebastien." It's the first time she's said it. I think we had an audience a moment ago. Hell if I know now because the rest of the world has ceased to exist. Nina loves me. I have never yearned to hear someone say that…until now.

"I, uh…I'm gonna, yeah." I hear Grayson speak, but it's a distant ringing in my ears.

"Mmhmm," I say right before my mouth crashes to Nina's.
We are outta here.

Somebody else can throw the rice…or is it birdseed? Who the hell cares?

"The sun has pretty much already set," I say as we reach the car and hold the door open for her. "I do know the perfect place to stargaze though. Trust me?"

She stands on her tiptoes to place a kiss on my mouth. "Always."

* * *

We ride the elevator up to my penthouse in silence, pretty much the same as the car ride over. My balcony is a perfect place to stargaze. I should know; I've avoided doing it for the last two summers. It's autumn now – chilly – but with a couple blankets and the heater on, it won't be bad.

I slide my key in the lock and as we enter, I watch Nina's eyes go wide as she takes in her surroundings. I take her coat and hang it on the hook. I shrug off my tux jacket and tie and toss them over the back of a dining chair.

Her eyes wander to the kitchen first. Yes, it's huge. Top of the line appliances that get used to make bacon and eggs as well as a blender for protein shakes. Other than that, the cook makes meals that go in the freezer for me to take out when I wish and throw them in the microwave or oven. I do make coffee in the morning for myself, but otherwise, the kitchen is pretty much just…a kitchen.

Three bedrooms, three baths, an office for my personal use. A living room with a massive fireplace topped with an enormous wall-mount TV because, well, football games…to watch from the sofa that could swallow a person whole – if they're not careful – and two very comfortable recliners. I also have a dining table but that's only used for poker games because what else would a single guy use it for? But the decorator said it's only fitting to put in a dining table, so I went along with it.

"When does your family come home?" she asks, eyeing me warily.

I blink fast and nearly choke. "My what?"

She blushes as her fingers twist together. "I-I thought maybe you lived alone."

Ah…Paris. Flats, apartments; families of four to five living in small spaces is common. Homes like mine are a dream where Nina comes from.

I take her hand in mine and lead her into the living room to take a seat on the sofa. Good God, she looks tiny, but so right, sitting on it. "Nina, I do live alone."

She glances around the room again, her eyes traveling from corner to corner, ceiling to floor and I watch as her face scrunches. "Don't you get lonely?"

"I'm trying to remedy that," I tell her. "Now all I need to do is convince her to stay."

"Why did you not come to me, S`ebastien?" Her eyebrows draw together and her mouth twists in disappointment, maybe pain.

"I did come to you, Nina. I was late that year," I explain. "I had the bar exam and Gray's wedding. I owed it Colton to get him away for a while because he was in a bad place and needed to get out of his head. He had been working so hard in school and was still behind Gray and me. I came to you as soon as I could. It was in August instead of June. You had moved two weeks before I got there. I missed you by two weeks. Your neighbor had no information, and I had no way to reach you."

Her eyes go wide with surprise before they fill with tears. "You came to see me?"

"I did." I nod, sighing. "Your neighbor said you had moved with your parents because there was a man they didn't want you with. I figured you had taken my advice and given your heart to somebody else." I raise my brows. "Apparently somebody your parents didn't approve of."

"Oh, S`ebastien," she sighs and drops her head in her hands. "You were that man. You can't give away what someone else owns. My heart has been yours for so long. Maman et papa could see how broken it was when you didn't come back. I had to tell them about you. We didn't have to move, but they thought it was best. I was accepted at Le Cordon Bleu and ma frere was accepted at Sorbonne. We all started over at the same time together." She reaches out and touches my arm lightly. "But I still waited for you."

I squeeze my eyes closed as my head fills with all the possible ways this could have been avoided. If I had left her my contact information, if I had let her know that I was coming later that year, left a message at the café, sent a gift with a note…all the things I could have done differently.

But you see, that's the thing – Sebastian Chambers is a selfish bastard. I took it for granted she would wait, always be there. I left after that last trip feeling sorry for myself – never once considering how Nina might be feeling. She was *my* conscience; I wasn't hers. And I have screwed my way through half of Essex Junction, Burlington, and every town in between here and Boston like a machine. I may be madly in love with her, but she deserves so much better.

I scrub my hands over my face in frustration and a good mix of self-loathing and hatred. "Nina," I whisper. "I'm no good for you. You have no idea what I've done."

She crawls onto my lap and straddles me, taking my cheeks in her hands and forcing me to look at her. "Did you love them, S`ebastien? Do you remember what they look like? Do you recall their names?"

She knows.

I gaze into the most beautiful brown eyes I've ever seen – the flecks of gold dance among the streaks of amber and green. Eyes that can bring a man to his knees with a single glance. Eyes that melt the organ I've sworn for years I don't have…my heart. She owns it.

"Not a one," I murmur.

She brings her mouth to mine and kisses me softly. "Keep your eyes closed, S`ebastien," she whispers against my mouth. "Do you love me?"

"More than I ever thought possible," I answer, my lips barely leaving hers, my eyes closed.

"Don't open your eyes yet," she whispers against my mouth again. "Tell me what I look like."

"Gorgeous amber eyes," I answer, stopping to take another deep kiss. "Long beautiful black hair that I love to run my fingers through, nine freckles on your pert little nose, seven on your left cheek, eight on the right, and the most kissable mouth." I kiss her again, my eyes still closed. "An appendectomy scar about three inches long and a mole that sits two inches left of the cutest little outty belly button I've ever seen. You look like my angel, Nina."

She whispers against my mouth, "You remember my name."

I open my eyes and study her face. "I remember everything about you. I've missed you so much."

"Show me how much, S`ebastien. Teach me tonight."

"No stars?" I ask, my eyebrow arched.

The playful smile she shoots me combined with the wink and tilt of her head causes a stirring in my belly and makes my manhood stand like a proud soldier. "Oh, S`ebastien, I plan on seeing stars. I'd like to start with the best part of Ursa Major." She giggles as she reaches for the front of my pants and slides her hand up and down my hardened length. "I believe you Americans call it your Big Dipper."

I growl as I stand with her in arms – her legs wrapped around my waist – and carry her to my bedroom.

* * *

She's here, in my penthouse – the first woman I've ever brought home. There's no fire under my ass, no itchy skin, no rashes, no anxiety, no rush. She's been in this room so many times over the last two years, in my thoughts, my dreams – whispering in my ear – only for me to wake up to an empty bed and empty arms. Not this time, I tell myself. *Not this time.*

Slowly and steadily I remove her clothing, one piece at a time. I've seen Nina unclothed before. I indulged her needs and cravings while in Paris the last time we were together – damn near killed me I might add – but this time is for both of us. My conscience niggles somewhere deep in my brain, but I shove it even deeper. She's forgiven me. I need to forgive myself and be what she deserves.

I back her up slowly towards the bed. When we reach the edge, she shakes her head before I can lay her down. "No, S`ebastien," she protests softly against my kiss, reaching for the buttons on my shirt. "You will be with me, your skin with my skin, your touch with my touch."

"Nina," I whisper as the touch of her fingers working the buttons loose and her peeling the shirt off my back sends ripples over my skin that make me shiver. I slip my shoes off my feet when she undoes the button of my pants and slides the zipper down. They fall to my ankles and I kick them off, socks included, and I'm left in my jerseys. I pull her close to me, leaning in for a kiss, moving us toward the bed again.

She places her hands on my chest, halting my movements. "All of it, S`ebastien," she murmurs against the kiss. "I have never seen you." She slides her thumbs into the waistband of my jerseys and slips them over my ass and around the massive bulge protruding from the front. I think they drop somewhere to the floor, but I'm not sure because I find myself ready to jet rocket into fantagasm as Nina wraps her hand around my dick and squeezes.

"Is this the correct way?' she asks – so damn proper – gazing at me with innocent eyes under a furrowed brow, awaiting instructions.

Drawing in a deep breath while removing her hand with mine, I nearly whimper, "A little too correct, baby."

I pick her up and lay her across the bed, not giving her another chance to protest, and place my knee between her legs so I can scoot her up where I need her to be before I hover my body over hers.

"We will fit, S'ebastien." It's more a question than a statement. I hear the apprehension in her voice. The confident woman from ten minutes ago has waned. She's trying to reassure herself as much as convince me. She's right, she never has seen me naked. And now that she has seen the Chambers rocket, she's either ready to go for the gold or join a convent. *Stay for the Olympics, angel.*

I gently brush the side of her nose with mine, kissing her softly. "We will fit, Nina, like a glove." I rock against her slowly, giving her time, waiting for her to grant me permission.

Her whimpers grow to soft pleas and moans. I enter her slowly, bit by bit, until I reach the barrier and hear her whisper, "More." I bury myself deep inside her, and still. I watch her face, hear her hiss, and see her mouth form that lovely "O" indicating pleasure. I smile on the inside, knowing we've reached the first plateau, and what's in front of us from here on out is going to be one helluva ride.

For the first time in my life, I make love to a woman. I put my heart and soul into it. And it feels incredible. She's incredible. She's…my Nina…my everything.

* * *

Watching her sleep; her hair spread out on the pillowcase, I want to reach out and run my fingers through it. Her face smooth like porcelain, flawless, the touch of pink in her cheeks. I count the freckles again. Yup, nine on her nose, seven on the left cheek, eight on the right. God, she's perfect.

I lost my head last night. The condoms in my nightstand were an afterthought. I have never in my life gone bareback. Guess it's true what they say…condoms really are like taking a shower with a raincoat on. I never gave it a second thought until our second time around. It's all copesetic. Nina was already on birth control in anticipation of finding me…nothing to worry about. Not that I was worried. Nina and I would make beautiful babies.

Would someone please tell me…where the hell is Sebastian Chambers?

I slip out of bed quiet as a mouse, grab a pair of sweats from the closet, use another bathroom so as not to disturb her, and make my way out to the kitchen where I start coffee. Then I perform another first for me. I make breakfast – for a woman who spent the night in my bed, in my home – and I realize I don't want her to ever leave. I look at the front door and smile. I don't want to open it and run; I want to double check to make sure it's locked.

Movement in my periphery catches my attention when Nina appears, wearing my tux shirt from last night. It hangs mid-thigh and otherwise swallows her whole. The sleeves are rolled, and it's buttoned so the open V falls between her breasts. Another first for me; I'm not alone. And nothing has ever felt so good.

"Good morning," I greet her, a fat grin plastered on my face. I scoot the skillet to a cool burner, shut off the one it was on, and offer a better greeting as I cross the room and pull her into my arms. "How did you sleep?"

"The way I've always wanted to." She tips her head back to look up. "In your arms. And it was perfect." She lifts onto her toes and pulls me in for a kiss. She tastes like my toothpaste. I don't know why the thought crosses my mind, but I'd like to think she used my toothbrush. Ten to one says she used her finger. Had it been anyone else, rest assured their own toothbrush would be dipped in toilet water before the next day. Just ask Grayson…nobody messes with my personal products.

"Yeah, it was," I whisper, squeezing her one more time. "Breakfast?"

"You cooked?" She nearly giggles as she takes in the kitchen. I don't think I did too badly. Eggs, bacon, coffee. Bachelor essentials. Shit! What was I thinking? She's a chef. She plants a soft kiss on my cheek and looks at me adoringly. "I would love breakfast, S`ebastien."

She eats every bite with a smile, adding a hum and a compliment here and there. I know it's bullshit, but it's funny and absolutely adorable.

We share a shower – me washing her, her washing me – Nina swearing she's not too sore for me to teach her more. I'm gentle, loving, slow…until she grasps my chin and orders me to stop treating her like a China cup. I truly think she means China doll, but who am I to judge? In any case, I understand. A second quick shower to wash off the education remnants and away we go. All in all, a thoroughly enjoyable morning.

Chapter 17

"I'll be back in two days to get Rufus"

"I volunteered before I knew what I was doing," I explain in the car on our way to pick up Briggs. "If I had known I had the opportunity to spend the entire day alone with you, I would have never offered to do this. I can still call and cancel."

"Don't you dare," she says. "They are newlyweds. We will have fun. But why are we looking at barnyards? Are they buying a farm?"

I laugh and proceed to explain, then explain we can't mention the dogs to Briggs or to Jana. This is a surprise, just to pass time and entertain Briggs, give Colt and Jana a little time alone before the trip to New York. I don't bother to inform her it was a ploy to make myself look good when the harebrained idea sprouted itself in my ass where my head happened to be planted yesterday.

I'm counting on Briggs to make Uncle Sebastian look like good husband and father material.

Yes, I know. I'm thinking of changing my name I'm so far gone.

* * *

"It's going to take you that long to get…ice cream?" Colt narrows his eyes and dips his chin, a wordless threat that no one else sees. He knows what I'm doing. We talked about it yesterday. He also knows Briggs will be primed and ready to get that "barnyard" by the time he and Jana are back from New York but, hey, what are friends for? Jana and Nina are busy getting acquainted and therefore distracted from the current conversation.

I called the breeder this morning and they will be waiting for us. Just wait until I talk to Briggs about getting a "rescue" dog as well. Wouldn't want that big ass barnyard to be lonely now, would we? Maybe a kitty too. Kindness begets kindness and all that. Colt's been eyeing a huge acreage on the lake anyway. He'll have room. The "Kinkaid Zoo" has a nice ring to it, don't you think?

I shrug casually and say, "We're looking to fill in some time." I wink. "Giving you and the wifey some time. We'll be a few hours." I extend my fist to bump it with Briggs'. "What do you say, buddy?"

He stares at my fist for a minute and looks to his dad, then to me and back to my fist again. "That's Uncle Tyler's code before we say corruption." He looks up at Colt with a sheepish grin. "And then we get in trouble."

I chuckle, but my mouth is fighting an evil grin picturing Colt and Jana throwing what I'm about to come up with. "Well," I say as I lay my palm out flat in front of him. "How about we have a code of our own and say 'conniption'?"

"What does it mean?" he asks.

"It's something people throw a lot when I'm around."

He thinks on it for a moment before he slaps my palm and nods. "Okay."

"Sebastian," Colt growls. Right about now I'm sure his biggest fear is Jana throwing a conniption, compliments of one Sebastian Chambers. Guess I won't be changing my name after all. I can be a lovesick fool and still be an asshole. Ah, life is good.

"Yes, Colt," I drawl, batting my eyelashes and feigning innocence.

He steps close, heeding a warning as he whispers, "You look, that's all. Jannie will kill me."

I hold my hands up in concession and promise, "No critters today, I swear."

We collect Briggs' car seat, get buckled in, and we are on our way to the breeder's – and probably a shitload of trouble. Between Nina and Briggs, I can't seem to find the word 'no' in my personal vocabulary.

And that is how I end up doing what I do.

"He won't stop licking my face," Briggs says as he giggles over and over while the bundle of brown and white fluff sits in his lap, paws on his shoulders, tongue lapping his cheeks, ears, forehead and nose. You'd think Briggs smeared steak juices on his skin before we arrived. The pup is already half the size of Briggs, his head the same size. Make that bigger than the size of Briggs' head now that I take a closer look.

"I told dad I wanted a dog bigger than me," he adds, looking at the woman who watches with glee. "How big is he gonna get?"

"Definitely bigger than you," she tells him, laughing. "And this little guy is the runt of the litter."

I eye her skeptically. "Don't the runts generally turn out to be the biggest in the end?"

She grins. "It's been known to happen."

"Uncle Bastian, I want this one," Briggs hollers as the puppy tackles him onto his back. I watch Nina sitting on the floor next to him, laughing and petting the pooch, ensuring the sharp little teeth don't sink into skin and cause damage.

"Briggs, we're just here to visit," I remind him, guilt consuming me as I observe the instant attachment taking place before my very eyes. "That's a conversation you need to have with your dad and mom."

"Mom's just gonna say no," he whimpers, letting the dog lick his wounds so to speak, as he sits himself up, his shoulders sagging.

"Why would mom say no?" I ask. "Didn't you talk about getting a dog?"

"Yeah," he sighs, his face scrunched in a frown. "But my time's not up yet. I still have to make my bed and put my dirty clothes in the hamper."

Oh the humanity.

Nina and I share a laugh as does the breeder. "For how long?"

He shrugs and grunts. "'Til mom says I'm done."

Hate to tell ya, kid. There is no expiration on cleanliness.

The breeder clears her throat and finally speaks up. "Well, maybe next time, but he really enjoyed you coming in to play with him today. He wouldn't be able to go with you today anyway, sweetheart. He has his final check with the vet tomorrow."

"Do we have to go?" Briggs asks, his eyes brimming with tears.

Nina places her arm around his shoulders as she eases him off the floor. "The puppy is probably worn out. We can go for ice cream?"

He pats the puppy's head and bends to hug him gently. "I really wanted to take you for ice cream. I'm sorry." The puppy trails after Briggs as he and Nina start for the door, nipping at his heels and yipping. He's already as tall as the kid's thighs. Briggs stops to hug him one more time, tears rush to his eyes and he whispers, "Bye Sammy. I'll talk to my dad. I promise."

Every hair on my body stands on end. No, I tell myself. I couldn't have heard that right. This has to be kismet. Halfway to the car, I hand the keys to Nina so she can unlock it and get Briggs into his seat. "I think I might have left my gloves inside. Can you get him settled? I'll be right back."

"S`ebastien, I don't think you had…"

"Please?" I quietly beg. She smiles knowingly and proceeds to the car while I go back and pound on the door to wait for the breeder to answer.

"Did you forget something?" she asks when she opens the door.

My balls, I think to myself, but instead I grin and say, "To buy the dog."

"You had better be calling for a reason other than telling me you have an extra passenger in that car," Colt answers the phone. No "hello", no "how's my son?"

I laugh heartily before responding. "Only three extra four-legged critters, Colt. That's okay, isn't it? He wanted six, but I talked him out of it. You should be proud of me."

"Chambers, this better be a joke."

"Get your panties out of a twist," I say. "I promised no critters today. We wanted to take Briggs to the burger joint for dinner. Is that okay?"

Please take note: I had promised him no critters "today". I made no pledges for tomorrow, or the day after, or the day after that, etc. etc.

I'll keep the pooch with me until after their trip to New York. Every kid needs a dog. And what better comfort is there when mom and dad are gone than a new best friend? Uncle Sebastian will present his gift when my *manny* duties start, and my rank of favorite uncle and asshole – next to Uncle Tyler – will forever hold its place. I don't have to pick up the dog until the day after tomorrow and that will give me time to pick up supplies, a leash and a collar and, from the sounds of it, a shitload of Puppy Chow.

Damn, I'm good.

* * *

It's not quite five o'clock when we reach the burger place – not too crowded. We find a booth and Nina slides in next to Briggs. As it was, she sat in the backseat with him to soothe his battered little heart after leaving the kennel without a dog. He's lucky she and I both speak French. I did not confirm nor deny buying the pooch, but I did manage to hold my tongue and not call Briggs a pansy for stealing my girl. It's bad enough I lost my afternoon alone with her, but in the end it is my fault and truthfully I am feeling pretty damn good about getting him a dog.

I'm bigger than Colt. I can take him. Once he sees that kid

with the dog, he's going to melt like a damn marshmallow. He'll love me as much as Briggs does…maybe. Ah hell, this is going to cost me dogshit duty for a year, isn't it? I'd better stop and buy a snow shovel while I'm out tomorrow night buying dog supplies. Do they recycle dogshit? I'll be digging holes to China for the rest of my life if I have to bury it. What do you do with dogshit? Maybe I should google it.

"Uncle Bastian!" Briggs shouts.

"Hmm?" I shake my head, bringing myself out of the dogshit dilemma.

"What are you gonna get to eat?" he asks. "I asked you like three times already."

Nina giggles. "He really did."

The waitress stops at the table, smiling brightly. Her voice holds the ever-familiar teasing lilt as she asks, "Hey, handsome. What can I get you?"

My brow furrows as I give her my best not-interested-do-your-job glance and answer without thinking, "Let's get their orders first, shall we?"

"I was getting their orders first," she snaps, narrowing her eyes. "A little full of yourself, aren't you Mr. Chambers?" She turns to Briggs. "Now, *handsome,* what would you like to eat?"

Briggs' heels thump against the wall of the booth seat below his feet as he swings them and he answers, "Um, a big chocolate shake with three cherries and two Oreo cookies on top."

The waitress laughs and Nina giggles as I give Briggs a stern look. "And how about some food to go with that sugar?"

His shoulders sag dramatically as he huffs, "Do I hafta?"

I slip my phone out of my pocket and hold it up. "Do I hafta call your dad?"

His eyes roll in contemplation and I swear I see a smirk. "Would it be just my dad, or would it be my mom too?"

Damn, this kid is good. Add to manny list: Threaten with mom. Colton is a pussy.

I look up at the waitress. Have I fucked her? Damned if I know. "He'll have a cheeseburger with fries. Just pickles. We'll dress it at the table." I look to the beauty across from me. "Nina?"

Nina orders and I follow. The best I can do is hope the waitress doesn't spit in my food.

"I really wanted the dog," Briggs says, licking the ketchup off his fingers. Yes, I had taken him in to wash his hands before the food came. I'm not an animal – outside the bedroom.

"I know, buddy," I sympathize. "He wouldn't have been able to leave today anyway. You heard the lady." I glance at Nina and she reveals nothing.

"I already had his name picked out and everything," Briggs says wistfully.

"You did?" I ask, needing to justify my purchase and ensure my hearing is intact.

"Yup," he says, so sure of himself. "His hair feels just like a girl in my preschool."

Starting early, but my kind of kid. Though I'm not sure petting girls' hair is school-approved. At least it wasn't when I was in school. They probably would have insisted on a Lenny test. Ass-slapping was my fetish so the rules may be different these days.

"Her name's Samantha but we call her Sammy." He nods his head, proud of himself. "He felt like Sammy."

My heart explodes. I do believe I just felt God pat me on the back and say, "Good job, Sebastian." Oh wait, that's the waitress, pointing out the ketchup I just dribbled on my shirt from the fry I hold halfway to my mouth. Damnit! She does have a low voice.

"Really?" I say, wiping the ketchup from my shirt. "I had a dog named Sammy when I was a kid."

"You did?" he asks, wide-eyed. "Was it a Saint Barny.. Ber.."

"Bernard," I correct him.

"Yeah, one of those."

"No." I shake my head. "She was a golden retriever."

He shrugs. "Any dog named Sammy would be a good one."

I smile, knowing I've done the right thing, regardless what anyone else says. "They sure would. Eat up, kid. We gotta get you back."

Nina's soft smile of understanding and pride makes a year's worth of dogshit duty look easy. I can't wait for next Friday when I present Briggs' new buddy to him. 'Sammy' the Saint Bernard.

It's not really Colt I'm worried about…it's Jana. So Colt will have to work a little harder at making her happy…more orgasms for the wife. How hard can it be? Win/win. He'll thank me later. Right?

* * *

"Or river!" Briggs shouts as we're on our way out the door.

Nina laughs and returns his goodbye. *"Au revoir, Briggs."* He was fascinated by her accent and had asked her to teach him some French words while dining. He mastered *"bonjour"*, for all of two minutes until it turned into "banjo" and now his goodbye has turned into a body of water. Between banjos and bodies of water, guests in their house will sit anxiously waiting to hear pigs squeal.

But, by God, his pronunciation of dog never wavered. Not only that; Nina taught him male dogs have a special pronunciation. *"Chien"*. Perfect.

* * *

Mondays are guaranteed court days for me, early, pensive, argumentative days…challenging. They'll have held them in the drunk tank, sometimes throughout the weekend, sometimes overnight, but fines and a slap on the wrist are never enough. I have a personal stake in every arrest, every violation. By the time I'm done, there will be a loss of driver's license; safety education classes to attend, community service to perform, and a fine hefty enough to cover the cost of a new car. One last caveat: the fine has to be paid before driving privileges are reinstated. Problem getting to work? Ask a friend, grab a cab, call an Uber, ride the damn bus. Lest we forget those two attachments to your ass called legs. Try walking–the thing my best friend couldn't do for nearly six months. If all else fails, grease your ass and slide awhile.

"Do you have to work tomorrow?" I ask, taking her hand in mine as we drive back to my place. I can handle some lack of sleep – anything for time with Nina.

"I do not work on Sunday or Monday," she replies.

"Stay with me tonight?"

"S`ebastien, what about your work?" She tilts her head and frowns. "You have early mornings, no?"

I smile, thinking of how much better my early mornings would be with her over all the sleepless nights I've had without her. "I'll be fine, even better if you're with me."

Her brow wrinkles before she replies, "I have none of my own clothes. I didn't pack any extras."

"Done," I tell her, and turn the car around at the next intersection to take her back to the apartment she shares with her cousin. We had stopped this afternoon before picking Briggs up so she could change her clothes but hadn't prepared for another night. This time, I'll have her pack some extras – you know – for a rainy day and any other I can possibly talk her into.

Chapter 18

"A Frenchie is not just a lovable little bulldog"

"Sooo…" Grayson smirks, "…who's the Frenchie?" It's 7:30 in the morning; I had to leave a warm, enticing Nina in my bed, and I have three cases sitting between a jail cell and the courtroom. Three cases, I might add, in which I need to convince a judge to either put back in those cells or slap an ankle bracelet on. Their cars have been impounded and I need to ensure those aren't released unless they're going up for auction or the fines are paid first. Two are repeat offenders, the other is a newbie to the system. There's one name on this list that already had my blood pumping and took two phone calls before I felt like I could breathe.

"Gray, I've got shit to do," I tell him, gathering papers and stuffing them in my briefcase as I head out the door. I'm due in court in half an hour and being late is not an option.

Gray stands with his briefcase in hand and follows me down the hallway. "I'll walk with you. I'd love to hear all about the Chamber tamer on the way."

I give him a side-eye. "Work, Kibbey. Focus."

He knows my moods and my taut jaw is a definite sign that now is not the time. "You'll tell me about her when we're done?"

I smile because, well – I can't help myself. It's real. It feels so damn good. I'm not in the courtroom yet. "Yeah, I'll tell you about her."

He shakes his head, laughing. "Damn, you got it bad."

"No," I sigh, anxious to get home to her, wanting to hear her say my name the way nobody else says it. "I got it good." I slap his shoulder, walking up the steps to the courthouse, grateful our office is only one block away. "Let's go get 'em tiger."

Did I tell you I play dirty? It may be arraignments, yes, but the judge and I have a long history. Relieved the young woman still lives here in Vermont and was willing to make the trip to the courthouse this morning – compliments of the car I sent to pick her up – it made for an interesting time in court. I love public defenders; so easy. The only reason his client qualified for one is because he lost everything he had in the lawsuit last year to the young woman who is now in a wheelchair due to the car accident he caused five years ago. I don't give a rat's ass that the accident was five years ago; that wheelchair she sits in is a lifetime sentence.

"Mr. Chambers," the judge addresses me as she leafs through the pictures set before her. "What am I looking at?" I want to scream that what she's looking at are the tangled remains of the car from which a dead man was extracted.

Instead, I keep my voice light and informative as I proceed. "Oh, those would show the results of the defendant's last drunken excursion behind the wheel, *that we know of*," I emphasize.

"Mr. Chambers," she chides.

I hold up my hand, pleading for a moment. "Ah, but I missed one, your honor. If I may, please." I nod to Ms. Black whose wheelchair sits in the aisle because – you know, wheelchairs can't fit anywhere else – and she moves herself forward as I scowl at the public defender as well as his client.

I smile at Ms. Black and step out beside her. "Ms. Black would be the other result. Permanently wheelchair-bound because the defendant decided to drive while inebriated."

The public defender clears his throat loudly. "Your honor, that case is over five years old. My client…"

"Over five years old?" I question/exclaim loudly and proceed before I can be interrupted. "Ms. Black, has your wheelchair gotten any more useful in the last five years? Has your quality of life improved so much as to excuse the defendant's driving while drunk again? Has your husband returned from the dead?"

Ms. Black knew what was coming. I forewarned her before she showed up. This asshole served under four years for manslaughter. He hasn't been out of jail a year and he's doing it again. His parole just ended and…here we are.

"Mr. Chambers!" the judge warns, tapping her gavel though not too hard. The judge and I have a short stare down before she flips through more pictures of evidence and papers in front of her. I catch her sneaking glances at Ms. Black, and I see her eyes soften in pity at the sight before her. Visual aids are a great thing.

Her gavel comes down hard. "Bail denied," she announces.

Yes! Last case of the day. My heart sings as I watch the court officer place the cuffs, none too gently I might add, and close my briefcase. Now to call his former parole officer and work out details that will make this asshole's life as miserable as possible. I walk behind Ms. Black's wheelchair as we make our way out of the courtroom, into the hall and over to the window that overlooks Lake Champlain.

"At least they got him before he caused another accident," she says, her voice low and solemn.

"They did," I reassure her.

"Molly!" A tall, well-dressed gentleman runs toward us and kneels in front of the wheelchair, taking her hands in his. He looks up at me. "What is this? I was just informed you made her come down here to face that animal. What the hell do you think you're doing?"

"He didn't make me do anything, Mike," she protests at the same time she tries to soothe him. "I came on my own. It worked, too. His bail was denied." She smiles up at me. "This is my fiancé, Mike Embers." The man ignores the introduction and tends to Ms. Black.

He fusses over her, tucking her hair behind her ear, palming her cheek. "Are you all right?"

"Better than I have been in a long time," she explains, a tear falling down her cheek. "He's going back to jail. I'm just sure of it. Mr. Chambers is going to see to it." She looks up from the permanent contraption that holds her body from morning 'til night. "Right, Mr. Chambers?"

I smile softly and nod. "If it's the last thing I do."

We bid each other farewell and I get caught in a short conversation with another attorney. When I reach the first floor of the building, I pause in the lobby, gazing out at the drive-up area for handicap access. I observe as Mike Embers lifts his fiancé out of her chair and into the car, buckles her into the seat, and closes the door before he loads the wheelchair into the trunk.

That right there is why I do what I do. I will not lose…I can't. People screw up – we all make mistakes. I can live with community service, huge fines, lengthy education, and loss of driving privileges for first-time offenders who haven't caused loss of life or limbs. Lesson learned: Call for a fucking cab! But repeat offenders? Fuck that.

* * *

"Okay," Grayson starts, sitting on the couch in my office, ankle over his knee, grinning. "Tell me about the Frenchie."

The day is nearly over, I've already packed up and I'm antsy to head out the door. With Colt gone for the week, leaving early isn't really an option. The courthouse closes at four o'clock, the filing of necessary papers has been done, communication with the parole officer was successful. All in all, a good day.

I arch a brow, inclining my chin. "The Frenchie has a name. Did she look like a bulldog to you?"

He holds back a laugh, but Gray never was any good at hiding a shit eating grin. "I don't know, Chambers. Looked like she could bite under the right circumstances." *He has no idea.* He bobs his eyebrows and mimics a light bark. He also has no idea how close I am to taking his head off.

"You done, asshole?" I grind through a clenched jaw. "Her name is Nina. I've known her for years." I close my eyes for a moment, reminiscing the first time I ever saw her.

"No kidding?" He shakes his head, chuckling. "Did you walk her to kindergarten? Put her on the bus?" He snaps his fingers as if enlightened. "I got it! You used to babysit her."

I pick up a pen and throw it at him. "Get out."

"Oh come on, I was being a smartass," he protests.

I point to the door, my voice a low growl. "Out."

"No," he says, his smile gone. "I want to hear about her. I've never seen you get all googly-eyed and kiss a woman before Saturday night. That's just…wow." He shakes his head, a sappy crease line between his brows. "That's not like you. It was kinda… sweet."

"Aww," I say condescendingly, waving my hand. "Look at you, all kinda…girly."

"Knock it off!" he shouts. "It's nice to see you have something for you. The last five years have been a bitch, Seb. You've put all your time and effort into Colt and this practice, and pretending…"

"What?" My head shoots up so fast, I think I pulled a muscle.

"You heard me." He sighs, leaning forward with his elbows on his knees. " I knew there was something going on; Colt and I both did. You were trying too hard. Work, eat, get laid, and sleep. You shut down when Colt got hurt and never seemed to recoup, you know? It was like your hatred for Jana seemed to spread to the entire female population for everything but sex."

He's right. I did use sex as a way to feel…something. It was a heartless, empty act that gave me a release of sorts, but was never fulfilling. I used work as a way to stay distracted…busy. I used Nina to remind me that somewhere deep inside I had a heart, a conscience, a soul. I also kept her a secret. I felt guilty knowing that somewhere on the other side of the ocean was a girl that made me whole. Did I feel better pining after something I couldn't have knowing Colt was doing the same? Sounds crazy, doesn't it?

"I got wrapped up in Kinzie and left you with a helluva burden, Chambers," he explains. "I'm sorry."

I scowl. "Colt has never been a *burden*. I can't believe you said that."

He sighs heavily, again. "That's not what I meant. I left a lot of it up to you to get him through the grieving process. Hell, I thought he'd get over her and move on. You never told me how bad it really was, how much he was still hurting after all these years. You've aged yourself carrying a burden that wasn't yours to carry. About damn time the weight came off your shoulders. Go live your life." He smiles slyly as he stands. "Just don't let that youngster give you a heart attack."

"You sonofabitch," I grouse, picking up my briefcase and heading for the door after him.

"Hey! Don't insult my mother," he chides. "How old is she anyway?"

"Twenty-one," I reply.

He turns, rubs his chin, narrowing his eyes while he scans me, scrutinizing. He pats my shoulder. "A little more exercise, better face cream. Give it some time. Maybe you can reverse the aging process."

I shove his shoulder to move him out the door and grumble, "Asshole."

He laughs loudly. "Give Frenchie a kiss for me." He tilts his head and grins. "Or is that give her a Frenchie kiss for me?"

One last shove and he's over the threshold. "Goodnight, Kibbey."

* * *

The penthouse smells so good when I walk in, I feel like I could lick the walls and savor the flavor. I had asked Nina to stay the day and make herself comfortable. Take a nice hot bath, read a book, watch TV, whatever made her feel good. Whatever made her feel *at home*.

The vision in my kitchen is one I could come home to

every night of the week, live with every day for the rest of my life. She busies herself at the stove, opening the oven once to check whatever it contains. Walking in the door set my olfactory sense on high alert but seeing what stands in my kitchen sends every other sense into overdrive.

She doesn't notice me watching her, didn't hear me come in. It's now I note the earphones and I'm captivated as she sways with the music, humming along softly. Two days ago, she was a memory I held in my heart and my head. Today she's here in my home. I can see her, touch her, hold her close. So I do.

I approach slowly, quietly, wrapping my arms around her from behind and breathe her in. She jumps in surprise and turns quickly, wrapping her arms around my neck.

"S`ebastien," she says breathily. *Nobody says my name like Nina does.*

I reach to pull the earplug out. "I missed you," I whisper.

"I missed you too," she replies, right before my mouth finds hers. She hums with the kiss – her soft plump lips taste like vanilla and a touch of mint. I'm home.

She tucks her fingers under the lapels of my jacket then reaches for my tie to loosen it. "You go get comfortable. Dinner will be ready soon."

"It smells fantastic." My face falls to a grimace as I suddenly remember what day it is. "Oh God. I forgot to tell you. Did…"

She interrupts with a giggle. "Your John and Clair come today? Yes they did. I am happy your Clair is a woman. I was in the bath when she walked in."

My lungs deflate and I pull her to me. "I am so sorry. I got caught up in having you here and then having to leave you and then court cases and…"

She giggles again. "S`ebastien. She was very sweet. She said you need a woman to teach you how to…" she looks puzzled for a moment and then says, "… drop a seat?" She tilts her head. "Your John is nice too."

I laugh, hard. *Oh, Nina. One woman says I need to drop the seat and one says I have a nice John. So many punch lines. So glad*

Grayson is not here.

I had been in such a state of oblivion this morning I had forgotten to tell her about the housekeeper coming. I had also neglected to inform her it was chef John's day to cook.

"How did you and *my* John do in the kitchen?" I ask, smiling.

Her face lights up as she animatedly explains, "He made sure I had all the ingredients for dinner, and I shared secrets with him about sauces."

My eyebrows nearly touch my hairline. Chef John is a pain in the ass. I don't even enter the kitchen when he's here. He's full of himself, hoity-toity, flighty as hell, but he knows his food and so long as he does his job, I keep him on.

"Wait a minute." I narrow my eyes. "You two were in the same room at the same time? He shared the kitchen with you?"

She nods quickly and laughs. "Yes. We turned the music up and danced while we cooked. We had so much fun. And then he asked me to marry him," she ends on another giggle.

I am in another world. This is what Nina does to people. She makes them laugh, sing, dance…Screeech!

"He what?!" I yell.

"Oh, S`ebastien." She laughs so hard she hiccups. "He's old enough to be my pere. At least my oncle."

"I'm going to go change," I grouse. The thought of her dancing with John has put a damper on my mood. What if it had been John that walked into the bathroom? What if John had gotten here first and Nina had walked through the hall naked? What if… what if…what if? What if I were to pull my head out of my ass and go get changed for dinner? I head toward the bedroom when I hear her whisper,

"S`ebastien."

I turn and see her sweet smile, the softness in her eyes that I note only when she looks at me. "I love you." *Damn, she reads me like a book.*

Three steps and I'm back where I was, with her in my arms. "I'll dance with you anytime you want."

"Even in the kitchen?" she asks, laughing.

"Anywhere, anytime, any tune." I begin to move her in slow, smooth dance steps sans the music – we make our own. I dip her and she giggles. See? Her laugh is all the music I need. Nina is all I need.

Chapter 19

Sammy the Saint Barnyard

"Okay, a collar and a leash." I furrow my brow, looking at the list in my hand. "And a harness I guess so the collar doesn't pull on his neck when I walk him. I also need a kennel, puppy food, some pee pads, treats, toys to chew." I roll my eyes. "Probably so he doesn't chew my shoes."

Nina laughs and shakes her head. "And everything else in the house."

I had my secretary make a list of everything I needed to pick up for the new canine to make for comfortable accommodations. The hesitant look on her face was enough to make me laugh, and cringe, but she took it in stride and performed the task without questioning when I told her it was for a friend. Technically… I can't guarantee Colt and I will be friends after the deed is done, but Briggs and I will be forever buddies and I am becoming rather fond of the little shit. He reminds me of me at that age. Actually, he reminds me so much of Colt at that age it's scary.

I pull out one of the kennels from the shelves and set it on the floor in front of me. It looks to be about the right size for little Sammy. Nina's chuckle turns into all out guffaws as she tucks the kennel back into the cove and pulls on my arm to lead me down to the rack of ginormous cages. The boxes alone that house the kits are nearly five feet tall.

"What…what?" I question.

"S`ebastien," she sighs. "He's only this size for a little while. He's going to be big." Her eyes go wide. "Really, really big. Like little horse big."

Colt is going to kill me.

I clear my throat, trying to remove the lump that has formed as well as the chokehold I imagine Colton or Jana squeezing around it. Too late now.

I nod with faux confidence. "Big it is."

My Hummer is loaded to the gills by the time we leave the pet store, and half the staff is waving goodbye at the door. Small wonder – I think I just bought half their supply. And tomorrow I get the dog. It has to be registered…it's a purebred. I don't know if they want him neutered. Not my call. The very thought of it is making my balls crawl back up into my body. But then, after Jana sees what I've done, I may be first on the list. I might never sleep with my eyes closed again. Damnit! Colt has a key to my penthouse. I'll have to get the locks changed!

"S`ebastien," Nina says, placing her hand on mine. "I should go home tonight."

I get a pang in my chest I've never felt before. I've never slept as well as I have the last two nights. I didn't wake up alone, she wasn't a dream, I only had to reach for her and she was there.

"Why?" I draw her hand to my mouth and kiss her knuckles. "You know you can stay. I want you with me, Nina. I can take you back in the morning before I go to the office."

"Bast, I still have my uniform to clean. I have to be in at ten o'clock to start to prepare the food." She sighs and I hear the frustration she tries to hide. "I live with Roz and I have a responsibility to her and to my job. I can't lose it." She shakes her head as she repeats herself. "I can't lose my job."

There's something in her voice that tells me there's more to this than she's letting on. *She can't lose her job?* Hell, I can take care of her. I understand her liking what she does – she went to school for it – she's not just a cook, she creates. But that's the sound of desperation in her tone.

I enter the parking garage, wait for the security gates to rise and pull into one of the three spots reserved for my vehicles.

"Okay," I tell her. "We'll get your things and I'll take you back tonight. Can we get a schedule straightened out?"

She doesn't answer with words, only nods and hops out of the Hummer before I can come around and help her down.

The ride in the elevator is silent. We hold hands and I swear I can feel hers tremble. Somewhere between the pet store and home, something's changed and I have no idea what it is.

We step inside my penthouse and I drop my keys on the counter, shedding my coat and hanging it on the back of a chair. I turn to take hers and see she already has it hung on the hook by the door.

"I don't have to leave just yet S`ebastien," she whispers. "I have a little time." She crosses the area to where I stand and wraps her arms around my neck, leaning in to place a gentle kiss on my mouth. "Always make the best of the time you have."

Before being given the full opportunity to consider the eeriness of her statement, she's leading me to the bedroom by gripping the front of my shirt while she walks backwards, lips locked to mine. Who am I to refuse the woman I love?

* * *

I'll never get enough of Nina. The way she moves, the way she moans and whispers my name. She's a quiet release – not a screamer. The way she quakes under me or over me. The way she bites her lip – better yet my shoulder – as she pants and every muscle in her body tenses when she squeezes around me. The way her eyes glaze over and become heavy-lidded when she's sated. The soft hum she makes and the smile that crosses her lips when her body is totally relaxed.

I don't want to leave this bed. Curling up beside her, holding

159

her for the rest of the night, and waking to my fantasy is all I want to do. Closing my eyes and shutting out the rest of the world has never sounded better, but unfortunately not an option.

"What time are you done tomorrow?" I ask, pulling her closer to me. "I can pick you up and you can go with me to get the pooch if you want."

"Ah," she laughs. "The chien for Briggs. How are you going to explain it to Colton and Jana?"

I lift one shoulder in a shrug, chuckling. "What can I say? The kid is convincing. He'll make a good attorney one day." I arch a brow. "Or a good con man."

She shoves my shoulder, giggling. "I think you have a big heart for little children and hate to admit it."

"Do you want kids?" I ask earnestly, and my heart sinks as I watch her gaze fall away from mine as she turns to get out of bed.

"Maybe someday. I should get ready to go."

My arm instinctively reaches for her and pulls her back. "Nina, what's going on? This isn't like us. Baby please, talk to me."

Her eyes are glassy with tears. "I don't want this to end."

"It's not going to end, Nina." I kiss her forehead, running my fingers through her hair and tugging her head back as I gaze into her eyes. "Ever." I lower my mouth to hers and savor my favorite flavor. She is the epitome of grace, femininity, softness. She is the rise to my fall. I will never let go.

For the first time in my life, I want to take a woman home to meet my parents. *Who am I?* I can see my mother bringing out the tape measure to check for birthing hips. Watch her nodding and smiling, picturing brunette babies with big brown eyes, dancing around the Christmas tree, a tiny touch of a French accent making them even more adorable than they already are. I can hear her asking Nina what her favorite flower is so she can call the florist to be sure they have them in stock for the wedding date; that which she will set in stone for ten days after she meets her. And every fucking thought makes me smile, because I'd do it too, sans the hips measuring. I know how good those hips are. I've covered every inch of them with my fingers and hands a hundred times.

"Have Thanksgiving dinner with me and my family," I say, out of nowhere.

She slowly shakes her head, her eyes wide. "I shouldn't. Roz and I will have dinner together."

"Bring Roz with us," I suggest, *out of nowhere*. Roz seems a little rough around the edges, but quite frankly, so am I. My folks are friendly people, they aren't likely to be put off by spikey rainbow-colored hair or nose rings. Ten to one says they've seen her at the country club a time or two. Maybe she'll tame down the brazenness for a day and if not, Briggs will find it entertaining.

Her eyebrows rise as she asks, "Your m`ere and p`ere would not mind?"

I laugh out loud, shaking my head. "No, Nina. They wouldn't mind at all." I pull her close and kiss her temple. "And they're going to love you."

* * *

"Does our age difference bother you?" I ask, my fingers grazing her knuckles softly as I hold her hand in the car on the way back to the apartment she shares with Roz.

She sighs wistfully. "Oh, S`ebastien. I waited three years for you to touch me in any way more than to hold my hand or kiss me. Then I waited two more years to feel you touch me again. So many times I wished on those stars. So many sunsets I wished you were with me to watch. I feel like I aged the difference in the time I waited. I love you like I've loved you forever and I love you like our story has yet to be told. Don't ever ask me that question again."

The train wreck that is me pulls over to the side of the road and slams the gearshift into park. I climb out of the car and go around to her side, open her door, reach over to undo her seatbelt, pull her out of the car and hold her so tight I probably put her back out of alignment or crack a rib.

"God I love you. I don't deserve you, but I'll do whatever I have to, to keep you."

"You can't keep me, S`ebastien," she sobs against my chest.

"I have to go back."

The air is sucked out of my lungs. "What?"

"I only have seven weeks left," she explains through tears and heavy breaths. "I am here on a work visa. It expires after the new year."

I rest my chin on the top of her head, the cold breeze chilling my cheeks the only thing I'm feeling. My body just went numb. She's a foreigner. Why had I not thought of it before now? Work visas are good for a year though. What the hell?

"Nina," I murmur. "How long have you been here?"

"I was in New York for nine months caring for my grand-p`ere and working. It was the only way I could stay." She sniffles, taking in shaky breaths. "I did web searches for you in Boston but found nothing. You don't have any social pages. When my grand p`ere died, Roz helped me search and found your law office here and I moved when I was able to get the job at the country club. I was going to visit your office, but you were at the wedding. I was going to find you before it was over, but you saw me first."

"I felt you there," I whisper. "I knew you were there before I saw you. I swear I could feel your presence, Nina."

I feel her nod against my chest. "That's how I knew to look for you." She tips her head up and attempts a grin. "It's not like you're hard to find. You are always the tallest."

Winking and forcing a smile, I reply, "Don't forget the best looking."

She breaks down again, her body literally racked with sobs, and I hold her tighter. "Nina," I comfort her, kissing the top of her head. "It's going to be okay. Did you forget what I am?"

"What?" she whimpers.

Feeling the emptiness as I take her shoulders and move her away from me so I can look her in the eyes, I remind her, "I'm an attorney. I work with a lot of attorneys who know how to deal with these situations. I'll fix this. You're not going anywhere. I promise I won't let you."

I know exactly what needs to be done and how easy it would be, but if I were to ask her to marry me right now, she would forever question if this were the reason why. I want to marry Nina because I love her, and I can't imagine the rest of my life without her – not because she needs a green card. I want to do this the right way – the legal way – so that when the time comes she can become a citizen in the three to five years it will take. My own dad can help me out with this, and will, because he's going to love her. Lest I forget, he loves me too.

"You can get me an extension?" she asks, eyes full of hope and tears.

I softly kiss each tear-stained cheek – taking a drop with each one – tasting the salt and sadness. "I can and I will. Trust me?"

"Always. I love you, S`ebastien."

Placing my lips on her forehead, an intimate gesture that I've grown quite fond of as of late, I murmur, "I know you do. I have no idea why, but nothing has ever felt so good. I love you too, baby."

* * *

"Sebastian," he answers the phone, surprised at my untimely call. "Everything okay, son?"

I suppose the call could have been postponed until morning, but I'm too anxious by the time I get home after delivering Nina. I want to get things in motion as soon as possible. Time is of the essence.

"Hey, dad." I sigh into the phone. "I need to talk to you about something, well, personal and I don't want mom…"

"Is everything okay?" I hear mom in the background, the worry in her voice apparent. "No one's hurt, are they?"

"No one's hurt, dad," I rush to tell him. "I just need you to leave the room. Tell her it's legal business, please."

He pacifies her in his usual tone with a chuckle. "No, no dear. Everything's fine. Just some lawyer questions. I'll be right back."

I hear shuffling for a few moments, and he chit-chats as he makes his way down the hallway I know so well and then I hear the sound of his office door as it closes.

"Okay, son. Who's the brunette?" He snickers. "I'll bet a dime to a nickel your mother has her ear pressed up against the door right now."

"The wh-what? Who?" I stammer.

"Hang on a minute." He chuckles before he reassures me, "We're clear. She's not sneaking around outside the door. I checked."

"Dad," I huff. "I need your help with an immigration case."

"Yes, I know," he says. "The French girl. I saw the way you looked at her. Saw the way you kissed her too."

The wedding.

"Uh, dad?"

"Yes, Sebastian," he drawls.

I sigh heavily. "I'm in love. Struck stupid, head over heels, can't hit my ass with both hands in love."

"You don't say," he drones sarcastically before laughing loudly. "The same girl from Paris a few years back?"

"How would you know about…"

"I'm your dad, Sebastian. I know everything," he says. There's no harshness in his voice, no judgment. It sounds more like…pride.

"I'd like to bring her for Thanksgiving," I tell him.

"Wouldn't have it any other way, son." I swear I can see his smile through the phone. "Although I think it might be best we get the paperwork underway as soon as possible. Get me the information I need and a picture. I can't meet her before your mother does though. I'm too old to sleep on the sofa and my back couldn't take it. The woman would never forgive me."

"I'm gonna marry her, dad." It's the first time I've ever said the word aloud and it feels good on my tongue; it tastes sweet. I realize the smile on my face is so big it hurts my cheeks, and I can't help myself when I laugh. "I'm gonna marry the shit out of her."

He laughs and says, "Use a little more tact with your proposal, but I'm happy for you, son. I'm really happy for you. Get me the info I need, and we'll get the ball rolling. We'll see you both at Thanksgiving."

"Um, dad," I hesitate. "She has a cousin that needs a place on Thanksgiving. Can I bring her too? She's a little different but…"

"Who? Roz?"

I gasp in surprise. "You know Roz?"

He roars with laughter. "Everybody knows Roz. If nothing else, she'll add a little color to the table decorations. I will admit, I'll never figure out how she blows her nose with those rings in there."

I groan, "Let's hope we don't get a demonstration at Thanksgiving."

"See you soon, Sebastian."

"Hey, dad?"

"Yeah?"

"I love you."

"I love you too, son."

If every kid could have parents like mine, the world would be a better place.

Chapter 20

"Just Us Guys"

Colton and Jana are due back Sunday evening. This leaves me with the next two days and nights caring for Briggs and… Sammy. No one else needs to know that. Grayson and Kinzie have had Briggs since Tuesday evening, staying with him for the last three nights. Briggs senior has had little Briggs during the day all week. Shockingly, Briggs senior does not look any worse for wear when I stop to pick up the little rug rat to perform my duties as the weekend manny. It was decided – not necessarily by me – that since Grayson and Kinzie were a team of two it would be best they take the weekdays, performing ritualistic duties of morning preps and meeting schedules. Weekends though? Lay in bed until you wake up, pizza and beer for dinner, football games and, *who in the hell needs a bath?*

"You ready?" I ask Briggs, picking up the duffle bag that holds his overnight things.

Briggs senior squares me a look of warning – and suspicion. "I can keep Briggs overnight if you have any plans for…" he clears his throat, "…extracurricular activities."

I shake my head, grinning casually. "Nope, no

extracurriculars, sir. Just us men this weekend."

He arches a brow and nods once. "Better be."

Briggs looks up in surprise, his eyes pleading. "What about Nina? Isn't she gonna come visit?" He looks to his grandpa. "She's really nice and she talks French. She taught me some words."

Briggs senior chuckles as he musses Briggs' hair and says, "That was nice of her." He looks to me with narrowed eyes. "You and Sebastian enjoy your men's only weekend and maybe she can teach you more words another time, okay?"

Little Briggs nods. "Okay." He turns to the door to leave and shouts, "Ah river, grandpa."

I whisper, "Au revoir."

Briggs senior snorts softly. "Goodbye, Briggs. See you soon."

"You're coming to my folks' house for Thanksgiving, aren't you?" I ask.

"I am," he replies. "Your mom called last week."

"Good." I smile proudly. "You'll meet my Nina then."

Colton's parents have been cut out of the family after the five years of torture his mother caused him and Jana. Five years of lost love, four years absent from a son he didn't know he had; all while she led people to believe Jana had abandoned him. Briggs senior having a great-grandson he knew nothing about. The lies and deceit were all too much. The dynamics have all changed. Once again, my parents step up to the plate and do their part in making sure everyone is included in family gatherings. Everyone who is welcome, that is.

"We need to stop at my place before we go to your house," I inform Briggs once we're in the car. "That okay with you?"

"Didn't you live with my dad?"

"Not with your dad, but I live in the same building your dad used to."

"Way up in the sky?" he asks, his hands high above his head.

"It is pretty far up there, isn't it?"

He shrugs. "I wouldn't want to jump out your window."

"Neither would I, Briggs." I shake my head, laughing. "Neither would I."

I had stopped home before I ran to get Briggs; just to change clothes, pick up my weekend bag, and throw Sammy's supplies into the Hummer. Since I had already put his kennel in the car, I thought it would be okay to let him run loose in the penthouse for the total of 45 minutes while I was gone.

Big mistake.

I slide my key in the lock and hear him yelp and start scratching. *Okay, so he's anxiously awaiting our arrival on the other side of the door, right?*

"What's that noise Uncle Bastian?"

"Think we'd better check it out, huh?"

Upon opening the door, not only is my nose filled with the scent of fresh dog shit, but there is a sofa pillow on the floor. Correction: the remains of a sofa pillow spread from one end of the room to the other on the floor. To top it all off, there is a large puppy looking up at us, tail wagging ever so happily, with one of my Ferragamo shoes, half chewed, hanging from his mouth.

Oh look, daddy! I brought you a gift!

Briggs' mouth is agape, his eyes bugging from his head, his breaths growing rapid as he stands stunned in the doorway. "Sammy!" he shrieks as he dives for the puppy. My shoe is a long-forgotten memory, for both the dog and me – as the puppy's tongue now finds it place on Briggs' face anywhere from his jaw to his hairline. I don't care about the shoe. I know there's a pile of dogshit to find somewhere, but I cannot take my eyes off the scene before me. I snatch my phone out of my pocket and hit the video record button. There is no way Colt can be pissed when he watches this. Briggs is so happy he has tears in his eyes. His giggles fill the room. Colt can get him a rescue dog. I got him his "Sammy". Do I feel a little guilty? Maybe. Enough to take the dog back? Not on your life.

"You gonna help me clean up his mess? You might as well get used to it," I tell Briggs.

"Yeah, dad told me I had to learn to clean up when I get

one. You can show me how." He stands and pats his leg, indicating for the dog to follow. "Come on, Sammy. Where did you poop?"

We find the pile. *Can you say holy shit?* Forget the snow shovel; they're going to need a damn bulldozer. The toilet…must put it in the toilet. In two separate loads, mind you. It only makes sense. Disinfectant. Be grateful it's not on the carpet. *Do not kill the dog, Sebastian.* We bag everything that deals with dogshit and set it outside the door so we can deliver it to the dumpster and wash our hands.

"Well, kid," I eye Briggs. "How do you feel about your dog now?"

"My dog?" His voice is shaky as he points to his chest.

I shrug. "Only if you want him. I mean, you did name him."

He takes a few deep breaths, letting the reality sink in. He wraps his arms around my legs and squeezes tightly. I think he's crying. "Thanks, Uncle Bastian. I'll take really good care of him, I promise." He sniffles.

I reach down and pick him up. "I know you will, Briggs."

"My dad's prob'ly gonna be mad at you," he sniffs, wrapping his arms around my neck. I have never held a kid in my arms. It feels foreign but good at the same time.

"Meh," I reassure him with a pat on the back. "I can handle your dad."

"Yeah," he says as he leans back from my arms and his eyebrows shoot skyward. "But my mom's gonna be *really* mad at you."

"I'll buy her some ice cream," I tell him. "That usually works."

"You better get us a new freezer too." His eyebrows furrow and he looks so serious as he instructs me, "Her favorite's Oobun Boobun and you're gonna have to buy her a lot."

I laugh out loud as I set him on his feet. "I'll be sure to remember that." I'm well aware that Jana's favorite is Ben and Jerry's Urban Bourbon. Something tells me news of the pooch is going to take more bourbon than ice cream though. Better make sure there's a good stash of both.

* * *

Briggs helps me get all the items in the house once we get there and we get settled in after taking Sammy out in the yard, watch him dump another load and pee in every spot possible. Jana's flowers are probably going to suffer every summer unless she puts an eight-foot fence around them, but by then their family should be moved into the house on the acreage Colton has been eyeing for them anyway.

"Okay," I clap my hands and take a seat on the sofa and pat the cushion next to me for Briggs to sit. He hoists the puppy into his arms and takes a seat next to me. The pup has had a good run in the backyard playing fetch – a useless effort – as it turned into a game of tug of war, so he settles in Briggs' lap with ease. I unfold the paper I removed from my pocket and hold it out in front of us to study. "No raisins, no grapes, no onions, no chocolate. Never share any gum. Those are all poison for a dog. No small toys where he can reach them, or he might swallow them and then…"

"He'll have to poop them out," he finishes for me. "Like I did the eraser I ate when I was little."

What the hell did Jana feed this kid?

I scratch the back of my head. "Uh, or worse. The vet may have to remove it. So let's keep all the toys picked up, okay?" I frown. "You ate an eraser?"

He shrugs. "I was chewing on a pencil in preschool, and it came off."

"So you ate it?"

"It was on accident." He shrugs again. "It didn't taste very good."

"I don't imagine it did." I chuckle as my phone rings. I hold a finger to my lips. "Ssshhh, not a word about Sammy. Okay? Our secret and it's a surprise," I tell Briggs before I answer when I see it's Colt calling. Why had I not thought about Briggs and phone calls?

"Hey, Colt," I answer the phone as calmly and casually as I

can. "How's Mr. Cooper doing?"

"He's doing really well," he says. "Back to giving orders instead of taking them, so that's a good sign. How's my boy? You don't have him drinking beer yet, do you?"

"Only root beer, Kinkaid," I laugh. "We're saving the whiskey for bedtime, so he'll sleep better."

"Glad to see you haven't lost your sense of humor," he says dryly. "Let me talk to him."

Pressing my finger to my lips in reminder of our secret, I hand my phone to Briggs.

"Hey, dad," he says into the phone. "Is grandpa okay?" The entire time he speaks with Colt, he pets Sammy, taking comfort in the puppy lying on his lap. The dog takes a deep calming breath and sinks a little deeper into his lap. I wish I had a video cam to record what I'm seeing now and show Colt how much comfort this canine is giving his son while they're away.

"Yup," Briggs says with a giggle. "He's being good. I'll tell you if he's naughty." He rolls his eyes. "I know, dad. I love you too." He hands the phone back to me. "He wants to talk to you again."

"He seems too calm," Colt says, his voice laden with suspicion. "What are you bribing him with?"

"What's that Briggs?" I feign conversation with his son. "You want to drive your dad's car again? Wiping out that mailbox was fun, wasn't it?" I laugh. "More chocolate and sprinkles on your ice cream? Sure, anything you want. Ooohhh, you like that redhead? Okay, I'll take the blonde. Just get her back by midnight."

"Funny man, Chambers," he growls.

"Oh, chill out," I chide. "Your grandfather is probably camped outside watching the house right now. He's scary, you're not. Now go have fun with your wife, relax and don't call again. We will see you on Sunday." I look to my little buddy next to me on the couch. "Right, Briggs?'

"Right!" he shouts, startling the puppy in his lap who jumps and yelps.

"Gotta go." I end the call as fast as I can, praying Colt

didn't hear.

"Sorry, Uncle Bastian," Briggs whispers, his face scrunched in a sorrowful grimace, the puppy now standing with his front paws on Briggs' shoulders, tongue lapping at his face. The kid is going to need three showers daily just to wash off the dog spit.

"No worries. You ready for pizza?"

His face lights up. "Yeah! No slimy things though," he warns, shaking his head.

"What are slimy things?" I ask, racking my brain…slimy things.

"Those yucky things that taste like boogers," he says.

I incline my chin and raise my brows. "And how would you know what boogers taste like?"

He shrugs. "I don't. That's what Uncle Tyler calls them."

Thank God. It's not my manny duty to teach him what is not included on the appetizer list.

I pull up my contacts.

Me: WTF are slimy things on pizza?

Colt: Shrooms, you idiot. Do you not know kid-speak?

Me: I know kid-speak. Half the time it sounds like Woof.

Colt: That better not have a hidden meaning.

Me: G'nite Colt.

Colt: Sebastian…

Colt: Sebastian………

I'm ordering the pizza online when I see his call coming in. I choose to ignore it, and again when it rings two minutes later. The puppy needs to go out to relieve himself. Wouldn't want any wet spots. I do text him later while we eat our pizza.

Me: Sorry, ordering pizza and taking care of Briggs is a full-time job. No time to talk. We're off to the bar now to get our whiskeys and women. See you Sunday.

The doorbell rings before Briggs and I finish our pizza. The puppy, thankfully, doesn't know where the sound is coming from so doesn't jump and bark, but his curiosity is getting the best of him as I clamber down the hall towards the front door. Taking a peek through the sidelight before opening it, I see Grayson, hands in his pockets, smug grin on his face, standing on the front porch. I consider ignoring him and going back to my dinner, but against my better judgment open the door instead – just a crack – holding my foot against the puppy so he doesn't slip past.

"Did you not see the 'no soliciting' sign?" I smirk.

"Oh, I did," he says cheerily. "I'm not selling anything." He winks. "It's a social services call, so to speak."

"What do you want, Kibbey?" I ask, my voice but a low growl. The puppy wrangles his way around my foot, seeking out new admirers, before I can stop him and jumps up to greet Grayson. Gray stares at the bundle of energy at his feet and then back up to me.

"Holy shit." His rumble of laughter starts low but increases rapidly as he bends to pick up Sammy. He nuzzles the dog to his shoulder and murmurs, "Somebody better tell me you're half grown, or I just lost one of my best friends because Briggs' mommy is gonna kill him."

I heave a sigh and open the door. "Come on." He walks in holding the bundle of fur in his arms, his coat collecting the loose hairs Sammy is shedding.

Lovely. Order the super Roomba tomorrow for Jana.

"Uncle Grayson!" Briggs shouts as he enters the room. "Do you like my new dog? Uncle Bastian got him for me." He walks over to take Sammy from Gray's arms. God as my witness, the dog is half as big as Briggs, but he has no trouble taking him and Sammy has no objections to being handed over. Briggs sets him down on the floor and they happily trot over towards the sofa where they both find a place on the floor to sit. We had a discussion earlier about keeping the dog off the furniture as over time he would end up taking up the entire sofa and mom probably wouldn't be too happy with that. Best to teach a young dog old rules.

Grayson watches them with fascination, then looks to me and mouths, "What the fuck were you thinking?"

I flash him a sly smile, my voice low. "I am now the favorite uncle. Top this one, asshole."

"Former uncles don't count," he mumbles. "You are *so* dead. *So, so* dead."

"Why are you here, Grayson?"

"Um, just checking to see how you guys were doing?" he says, shrugging. "Spreading the Grayson charm around."

I close my eyes, take a deep breath and count to ten silently. "Once more, why are you here?"

He huffs impatiently. "Fine. I was asked to *check in* on you guys. Just to make sure things were going well."

"Colt wanted you to check on us? On me?" I sneer.

"Hell no." He winces as his shoulders sag. "Kinz wanted me to see if you guys needed anything."

"Would you go home and knock up your wife, please?" I glower. It wasn't a request, and he knows it. "And if you say one word about the canine, you will find yourself incapable of knocking up your wife." I hold up a finger. "Wait there."

I run to the kitchen and pull the Dust buster out of the charger and walk back to where he stands, turning it on to vacuum the dog hair off of his coat.

He shakes his head when I finish, looks at Briggs and the puppy playing on the floor, and whispers, "Dead, Seb. You are *so* dead." He laughs as he heads toward the front door. "See you later, Briggs." He turns one last time to me. "I'd say see you Monday, but…may take a few days to get your funeral plans arranged." He pretends to shiver, makes his exit and closes the door behind him.

* * *

She answers the phone with a breathy whisper, "S`ebastien." It's the voice I've needed to hear all day. It lets me breathe a little deeper, feel a little stronger, relax a little more. I finally got Briggs to bed and now have the time to devote to Nina.

I instantly respond with a hum before I ask, "How was your day?"

"My day was fine, but I'm guessing yours was more interesting. How does Briggs like his Sammy?"

I wish she could have seen it. I wanted her to be with us when he saw his dog for the first time; to share that happiness. God, I want her with me for everything.

"He loves him already." I chuckle. "He snuck him into bed with him. That dog takes up more room than he does. I know I should take him off the bed, but I just can't bring myself to do it. Not tonight."

She giggles – the sound of which is music to my ears. "You are such a softie."

"I am. I admit it," I concede. "A softie for you too."

"Not always, S`ebastien," she teases. Three days without her. This right here feels like penance. I need Sunday night. Colt can ream my ass on Monday after court cases. I don't want her around for the fallout when they get back, but I can sure as shit have Sunday night with her.

"Stay with me Sunday night? I'll pick you up as soon as I get done here?"

"I'll wait for you to call," she replies. "Good luck."

"Nina," I whisper; her name rolling off my tongue like a melody. "I love you."

"I love you, S`ebastien. Step outside and look at the stars with me."

I stand to walk out the backdoor. Looking up at the clear dark sky, I take in the vast array of stars shining brightly, blanketing the sky with the memories that held me together in the times we were apart. I smile to myself.

"Do you see it?" I whisper. "The Big Dipper?"

She hums softly as if appreciating the sight before her. "I

see it."

"Find it, Nina. Off the tip of the ladle," I instruct her. "The bright one. The one we shared, no matter where we were."

Her voice is so soft I barely hear her. "I see it, S`ebastien. I've always found it. And now I've found you."

The swell in my chest is almost too much to take. She relentlessly searched for me until she found me, and I am never going to let her go again.

"You're not going anywhere, Nina," I tell her. "I promise you. We'll be looking at these stars together forever, okay?" I know my dad. He won't let me down.

She sounds hopeful yet still unsure. "Yes."

"I love you," I reassure her. "I'll see you Sunday." I end the call and take a breath, blowing it out slowly.

If not for sunsets and stars…

I look back up to the sky one last time. The North star shines and twinkles. I swear it winks at me. It's like a big diamond that stands alone up there in the…

What the hell am I thinking? Briggs and I have some shopping to do tomorrow.

Chapter 21

"Because he named him Sammy"

"Ah, Mr. Chambers," the sales associate at the jewelry store greets me with a provocative smile as we walk in the door. "So nice to see you again." She then notices Briggs by my side and eyes him skeptically before smiling at him and sneering at me. "And you brought your son this time?"

Briggs doesn't hesitate to answer. "Nope. I already got a dad. Uncle Bastian got me a dog and now he's gonna get Nina a ring. She speaks French and she's really pretty."

She chuckles at his precociousness and narrows her eyes at me. "Well, Nina's a lucky girl."

Sonofabitch. I banged this sales associate back when I bought Nina's necklace and earrings. How could I forget that? Because she was forgettable…just like all the others.

"Would Nina be the one who wears the necklace and earrings as well?" she asks, the ring of jealousy in her tone that tells me the one-off that night is like the hundreds of others I would give anything to take back.

Okay, she either wants the sale or she doesn't. Like everything else in my life, this is going to take time to get past.

Nina is my future, my sins are my past. If she can forgive them, I don't give a rat's ass what the rest of the female population thinks.

"She is," I reply coldly as I nod toward the display cases. "So only the best for the best. Think you can help us out or do we need the manager?"

She retreats into sales mode and paints on a flat smile that makes me wonder if she's hiding fangs or suppressing gas. "I'll be happy to help, Mr. Chambers. Do you know what you're looking for?"

"A big one!" Briggs exclaims. "My dad says size matters."

I pinch the bridge of my nose and hold back a laugh as the sales associate grumbles indecipherable words on her way down the counter.

Size matters. Hmmm...that line ought to come in handy tomorrow night when his dad meets Sammy. Let's not forget to stop and get bourbon for Jana. I wonder if I can talk Colt into getting her good and drunk on the plane ride home.

* * *

"I get him first," Jana grinds through a jaw clenched so tight I'm afraid she might break some of those beautiful straight white teeth.

Colt holds her off the floor by the waist while she kicks and bats her arms, trying to get to me to use as her punching bag. Briggs is in the living room playing with Sammy while the *adults* have a discussion in the kitchen.

"I'll kill him for you, baby," Colt whispers. "I know where to bury his body. If that doesn't work, I'll cast his feet in cement and throw him into the waters of Lake Champlain. He'll never be found."

While they discuss what to do with my remains, I fish around in my pocket, dig out my phone, and pull up the video of Briggs' initial meeting with the pooch and hit play. I lay my phone on the counter and wait as the sound of his giggles fill the room and watch as they lean over the counter, eyes pinned to the small screen in front of them.

"He named him Sammy," I murmur as the video ends.

Colt's head whips toward me, his eyes filled with wonder. "After . . ."

"Nope," I answer, my eyes misty. "He had and has no idea. I couldn't say no, Colt." I look him in the eyes and see them glass over as the shadows of memories take hold. I shrug, shaking my head and repeat slowly, "I just couldn't say no."

You see, Sammy wasn't just my dog. She was a therapy dog for Colt as well. He had such a shitty life at home – parents that were too busy being socialites and ass kissers – that he needed that extra touch of companionship too. And that is where Sammy played a role. Sammy taught Colt gentility, would never tell his secrets, gave him some responsibility, and taught him unconditional love… just like she did with me. She fetched our baseballs when we practiced at the park. She waited at the damn door every day until we came back from wherever we'd been, slept at the bedside every night. And when Colt had bad dreams, she would sneak up into his bed and sleep beside him. Colt and I both stood at the vet's table at her side her when it was time to put her down; hardest thing we've ever had to do. We were eighteen, high school seniors. Cried like babies. Sammy was one helluva dog.

Colt sets Jana on her feet, slides his arm over her shoulder pulling her tighter to him, and kisses her temple. "We'll make it work, baby. Big house, big yard, ten kids. Remember?"

"Ten?" she whines.

He winks and smiles. "Only if they're good looking."

"Dad!" Briggs yells from the living room. "Sammy just puked." I'm not shocked; he does have a tendency to eat fast. Little porker. Should have done half portions at a time. He's due to go out as well.

Jana waves her arm toward the living room and growls, "Looks like your manny duties aren't over yet."

I smile and head for the cupboard under the sink to grab the disinfectant spray. "Happy to be of service. By the way, the deluxe model Roomba will be here tomorrow." I stand once I've found the spray and take a bow. "You're welcome."

She glowers. "Roombas do not clean up the other messes dogs make, Sebastian."

"Sammy has not had an accident all weekend," I proclaim, puffing my chest a bit too much because as I do we hear Briggs holler,

"Mom!"

Damnit! Should have taken him out before our discussion too. I have got to get out of here.

* * *

Nina rushes out, bag in hand, before I get to the door to knock. She drops the bag, jumps into my arms and plants a kiss on my mouth that makes me forget where I am, who I am, and that there's a world outside of this little bubble in which I'm standing.

"Is Colton still your friend?" she asks, brushing her hands down the front of my shirt as if checking for injuries.

It takes me a moment to realize she's asking about Sammy. I chuckle, recalling Colt's reaction. "Yes, we're still best friends, actually. Jana?" I wince and hold my hand up, tilting it back and forth. "Hmmm, maybe not so much. She'll get over it. You ready to go?"

"I am all yours, for all night," she says, smiling. And I am all hers, for all eternity – if she'll have me.

Instead of driving straight back to my place, I drive down toward the lake – strategically parking on the far side for the view that I'll need for the plan that I have. The air is more than crisp tonight. The leaves crunch under our feet as we make our way toward the lake and the benches that line the edge. Our breaths leave a trail of white steam with every exhale against the cold night air. Nina doesn't question why we're here – just walks beside me, neatly tucked under my shoulder with my arm wrapped around her. It's quiet, peaceful – a few bird sounds as they ready themselves to settle in for the night, a scamper of wild ground animals as they make their way toward their burrows, the water lapping the edges of the lake due to the breeze. Otherwise, it's just us.

We take a seat on a bench at the edge of the lake, and I spread the blanket I took from the car and spread it over our legs for warmth. I feel my jacket pocket again to ensure the little black box is safely tucked inside. It is. We sit back and relax, watching the sky for the bright lights to appear as the background grows darker by the minute.

"Find it for me, Nina," I say after the sky is dark.

She points her finger high and traces the Big Dipper from the tip of the handle, all the way around the bowl, and then back across the upside-down portion until she reaches the tipped corner of the ladle. She then follows that point in a straight line down to the star she's looking for.

"Right there," she whispers then follows with the same words as always, "so bright it sparkles."

"Just like the girl who found it," I tell her, my voice low. I open the box and hold it up. "And so does this." I drop to one knee in front of her. "I can't change who I was, but who I am is the guy who loves you more than I knew possible. And if you'll have me, I promise to do my best to make you happy. I'm no prize and I know I'm getting the better end of this deal, but…"

"Are you done?" she snaps, her voice tight, eyes narrowed.

My chin drops to my chest as I heave a sigh. *Rejection at its worst.* "Yeah." I start to rise, and I feel her hand seize my shoulder and push me back to my knee.

"Stop trying to talk me out of it before you ask me," she scolds.

My eyes search hers and I see a spark of amusement as I watch a slow smile hitch the corners of her mouth. I should have known – self-deprecation was not the way to go about this. Man, I really suck as an attorney outside the courtroom.

"Nina Lafon," I whisper, "Will you marry me?"

"Yes," she squeaks, throwing the blanket off as she leaps forward, tackling me to the ground, straddling my hips. "Yes."

"Park closes at ten." The angry, commanding voice comes out of nowhere as the flashlight shines bright in my face. "What are you kids doing out here? A bit chilly, don't ya think?"

Nina falls forward and giggles against my chest and I groan, "Just getting ready to leave, sir."

"That you, Mr. Chambers?" He steps closer, the light blinding my vision completely. Not only is he surprised but apparently ready to piss his pants as his voice quivers, "I-I'm sorry, sir. I thought you did these things in the privacy of…"

"Turn off the damn light, Duggan," I growl, now that I recognize his voice. "I'm not doing anything illegal. Jesus, I'm not a pervert."

Once again, my reputation precedes me wherever I go. The stout, young security guard from the courthouse presumes I'm out in the park by the lake getting my rocks off when it's 30 degrees outside. Admittedly, there was a time I could probably have done it in an ice bath, and frankly, I would be more than willing to take Nina under the stars covered by the blanket. But seriously, I have every amenity at home and a nice warm bed that I prefer over getting crunchy leaves and mud up the crack of my ass.

"I…I'm sorry if I interrupted, sir," he stutters. "I didn't know…"

"Just shut up a minute," I command. "I'm on a mission here. Let me finish." I take the ring from the box and place it on Nina's finger. I grasp the nape of her neck and pull her in for a kiss she won't forget, because this is everything. "I love you," I whisper when the kiss ends. I look into the eyes that I want to wake up to every morning for the rest of my life. The eyes that seem to see in me what I never could. "You own me, Nina Lafon. Let's go home."

We rise to our feet and I grab the blanket from the bench.

"Duggan," I say with a smile. "Meet my fiancé, Nina Lafon."

His eyes flit back and forth between the two of us. It's dark, but there's enough light from the moon to cast a dim glow and if he shines that damn flashlight on me one more time, I'm going to shove it up his ass.

"You're engaged?" he gasps. "That's, that's great! Gonna break a lot of hearts…"

"Say hello, Duggan." I roll my eyes, staving off the temptation to punch him just to shut him up.

He extends his hand to shake Nina's. "Congratulations, ma'am. Mr. Chambers is a really nice man. He's tough in the courtroom. Puts away a lot of bad guys . . ."

"You moon-lighting, Duggan?" I interrupt his attempts at brown-nosing, looking around the park. "Short on cash? State doesn't pay you enough at your day job?" I eye the parking lot where my car sits and see the labeled 'City Parks' truck sitting next to mine. He seems legit. One never knows these days though. Doesn't mean I won't be double-checking tomorrow. Abuse of authority is intolerable.

His eyes go wide as he holds his hands up in defense. "I okayed it with my supervisor. It's only three nights a week. My girlfriend and I are saving for a down payment on a house. By spring we should be all set. I only work until eleven and the only night that mixcs with my regular job is Sunday. I go straight to bed when I get done and I'm fresh as a daisy come Monday morning."

I chuckle as he rambles. "Duggan, it was a simple question." I'm not nearly as concerned as I was minutes ago. Checking with his supervisor is as easy as a phone call and he knows it. He probably also knows I'll be doing it.

"Well." I slide my arm over Nina's shoulder. "We'll let you get back to work. I'll see you in the morning." I grin and tip my chin, throwing his words back at him, "Fresh as a daisy. Goodnight, Duggan."

"Goodnight, Mr. Chambers…and future Mrs. Chambers," he says with a laugh. We start for the car – Nina tucked under my shoulder where she fits so perfectly – and halfway there I hear him call out behind me. "Can I tell the guys at work about this?"

"Wouldn't expect anything less, Duggan." I turn one last time. "Just make sure you tell them how damn happy I am."

* * *

"Are you hungry?" I ask once we've gotten our coats off and

hung up. I can't stop staring at the ring on her finger. It's perfect; a solitaire, three carats, not too big, not too small. I want to take her to the jeweler so she can choose the jacket to make it a wedding ring. Once I heard Duggan say future "Mrs. Chambers" I realized I want it now. It fits her. Lafon is a nice name – French, pretty. But Chambers would look good on Nina. I want to see her sign it in her own handwriting. I want her to have it tattooed on her ass so I'm a permanent fixture. Cham on the left cheek, Bers on the right, *"here I am, stuck in the middle with you". I shake my head to knock the Stealers Wheels tune loose. Not the time, Chambers.*

"S`ebastien," she inquires, tilting her head. "Where are your thoughts?"

"You said yes," I whisper, taking her in my arms, brushing my nose against hers ever so softly. "No take backs," I murmur before sealing her mouth with mine in a kiss that lasts all the way through carrying her to my bedroom, my arms around her waist, her legs wrapped around mine.

* * *

"S`ebastien," she moans as her top half rises off the bed so our bodies meet at every possible point, skin on skin, every sensation seeking its mate. She's so intense as her teeth sink into my shoulder – not so much painful as it is erotic. I love the little marks she always leaves behind. Her nails scrape along my back as she holds herself tighter to me. "There," she whispers as her hips move in sync with mine. "Right there." She clenches around me, trembling with her release. Her thighs squeeze my hips and her heels dig into the backs of my thighs. She's not a screamer; no Broadway productions of orgasmic bliss. It's intensity I don't need to hear because I feel it right down to my very soul. A heat that runs through my blood, my bones, and most importantly – my heart.

She spurs my own release – exquisite pleasure I've never felt before her – knowing I've given her the same. The euphoria goes on forever, draining me of all thoughts of anything but Nina. She's my drug, my drink, my sustenance, my mere existence.

I was such a fool for ever thinking she was my symptomatic treatment, a fix, my Band-Aid, when all the while she really was my cure.

I drop to my elbows, spent from the workout, but ready to go again if she so desires because, well – she's my Nina.

Chapter 22

"Mom, will you please stop crying?"

The snow has been falling softly since this morning, so the Hummer is the vehicle of choice for the day.

Roz climbs into the backseat and lets out a loud whistle once settled. "Nice wheels, Baster. Did you bring me any diamonds? Always up for a little stud for my nose. You know, just tossing out some Christmas ideas."

My lips tip in a smirk as I soak in that little tidbit of information and I toss her a nod as I eye her in the rearview mirror. "I'll keep that in mind, Roz."

"Could also go for a big one for the belly button." She crosses her arms over chest and shudders. "Leaving the nips alone though. Those suckers hurt."

"That's a little TMI," I mumble then ask, "You ladies ready?"

"Ready," they answer in unison.

The front door opens before we reach the threshold. My mother's smile stretches from ear to ear as she bounces on her toes.

"You're finally here!" she proclaims, absolutely giddy with happiness.

"Hey, Mrs. C," Roz greets her, holding up the bag housing the homemade pies Nina insisted we bring. "How ya doin'?" She tips her chin to my dad. "Mr. C. How's it hangin'?"

Real country club charmer, this one.

The façade of crystal, silver, and China etiquette has come off and the personality of pink, purple, and turquoise hair accompanied by three nose rings and an eyebrow bar makes its appearance without fanfare. I was pleasantly surprised when Roz chose to wear a dress and heels versus her usual combat boots and camouflage pants. She dresses per the uniform code at the club, but once work is over, the real Roz appears – a tiny packet donned in military garb, decorated with colorful tats, topped with shiny baubles. The perfect mix of a Ken and Barbie doll you never want to play with, for fear she could end up Chuckie by the end of the day.

"Rozalyn," mom cheerfully returns her greeting and pulls her into a hug. "I am so happy you could make it."

"Hey, mom." I lean down to give her a hug. "Happy Thanksgiving. Got somebody I'd like you to meet."

I turn and wrap my arm around Nina's waist, tucking her close to my side. "Mom, this is Nina Lafon."

I see my dad standing in the background; hands in his pockets – an encouraging, peaceful smile on his face – and he nods and winks. It's all I need. I can breathe a little deeper, smile a little broader.

Tears streak my mom's cheeks as she studies Nina's face. Her hands are clasped as she holds them tucked under her chin. "She's so beautiful, Sebastian."

I chuckle softly. "Mom, she's standing right here."

"Oh," she startles, coming out of her initial shock. "She is, isn't she?" She scoots me away from Nina with one hand and launches herself forward to hold her in her own arms. She rocks her back and forth as she squeezes. She sniffles, catching her breath between semi sobs.

I look to my dad, heave a sigh, and groan, "You told her."

He shrugs casually. "You think this is bad. You should have

seen her two nights ago." He laughs and shakes his head. "Told you that damn sofa was uncomfortable. I wasn't taking any chances."

I try to loosen my mother's embrace on a deer-in-the-headlights frozen Nina. "Mom," I soothe her as I take her by the shoulders and gently pull her back. "Mom, she's gonna be here the whole day. Unless of course you smother her and then we'll spend it at the ER."

"I'm-I'm so sorry, dear," mom stammers. "It's just Sebastian's never…"

Don't say it mom. Please don't tell her I've never brought a woman home.

"It is all right, Mrs. Chambers." Nina giggles and reaches out to soothe her with a soft touch to her shoulder. "I have looked forward to meeting you as well."

"Oh," mom whimpers, her hand over her heart. "Your voice, your accent."

"Mom." I roll my eyes. Good grief. The woman has traveled the world, heard a hundred accents. She, herself, speaks French!

Finally, my dad takes charge of the room. "What do you say, Roz? Shall we go toss back a few and get this party started?"

The doorbell rings and the Kinkaids arrive; party of four. Colt, Jana, Briggs and Sammy. Soon after we are joined by Grayson and Kinzie, followed by Briggs senior.

"Is your brother going to make it?" mom asks Grayson.

I freeze and do a double take. "Tank is in town?"

Grayson laughs and nods while Kinzie rolls her eyes and sighs. "Yeah," Gray says. "He rode that damn Harley in the middle of winter in Vermont! Can you believe that shit?"

Mom huffs, "It's not the middle of winter, Grayson. It's not even the end of November yet. We've got months to go. What's that boy going to do?"

"Dad's going to loan him a car while he's here, I guess," he says with a shrug. "Or I can always loan him one of ours."

"You wouldn't!" Kinzie growls.

His head whips in her direction as he scowls. "He's my little brother, Kinz. Of course I would."

She visibly shudders and grumbles, "Just make sure you get it cleaned afterwards. I don't want to sit in the McDonald's leftovers he spills on the seats. I sat in ketchup the last time and everybody thought I started my…"

The room fills with laughter and the doorbell rings before she can finish scolding a non-present brother-in-law.

You would think my mom forgot she has her own son when she opens the door and flies into the arms of the six-foot two giant in front of her. Scruffy jeans embellished with holes, a chain wallet, combat boots, leather jacket, short-ish hair that never looks combed but falls right into place, and a face full of scruff. Meet Tank Kibbey, ladies and gentlemen. Military hero, voice full of gravel, and major player.

"Tank!" My mom's shrill scream rings throughout the room as he picks her up and twirls her around. She giggles like a schoolgirl as she says, "Put me down."

I look to Grayson and smirk. "Couldn't just go to law school like the rest of us."

"Ahh," dad says, rounding the corner to join us. "The Tanker must be here."

Roz rounds the corner right behind him and her eyes go wide as her brows shoot skyward, taking in the mass of muscle and blue eyes in the doorway. She takes a few more steps forward before she pauses next to me and whispers, "Sweet Jesus. My seat better be next to him."

"Sebastian's getting married!" mom declares, wiping her cheeks again before Tank can get the door closed behind him.

All eyes turn toward Nina and me. Colt's and Gray's faces light up with amused smiles as they stare at me. Jana and Kinzie rush to Nina's side to inspect the ring.

"Yeah, yeah, yeah," Roz mumbles, taking a sip of her Manhattan. "Old news. You get me a seat next to him at the table and I won't tell mummy you've been bangin' my cuz at your penthouse."

I glower at her. "Some things are considered sacred, Roz."

The evilest laugh I've ever heard rumbles from the pint-sized kewpie doll standing next to me. "And some things come in handy for blackmail, Baster. Get me the seat."

"Roz," mom calls as she walks Tank toward us, a gleam in her eye that I've only seen when she's introduced women to me. "I have someone for you to meet."

"Kinda hopin' it's that luscious hunk of man you got hanging on your arm there, Mrs. C," Roz sasses as her eyes flare with heat.

Roz is living proof: Putting a woman in a dress does not make her a lady. Apparently it only makes her horny.

My mom giggles as she pulls Tank along. Tank arches a brow as his eyes peruse Roz from her head to her toes and back up again. Not that it takes long; Roz is tiny. It's like a small town; blink fast and you've driven through before you ever know you were there.

There is no doubt in my mind there is a seat at the table next to Roz set special for Tank. My mother knew exactly what she was doing before this day started. Good thing Briggs has Sammy, or she would have probably invited one of the neighbor girls over for him.

She performs a proper introduction, though totally unnecessary. These two had already eye-fucked before they shook hands. When mom is done she turns to me, grabs me around the waist – because she's too short to reach my shoulders – and starts to cry again.

"My boy is getting married," she weeps into my shirt. I hug her back and gently squeeze her shoulders.

I chuckle softly. "Yeah I am, mom."

She releases my waist and reaches for Nina and pulls her in so we're now a huddle of three. "And you," she sobs against her. "He's marrying you. You're just perfect."

"Mom," I groan. "Will you please stop crying?"

"Let her cry, S`ebastien," Nina whispers as she looks at me and I see tears in her eyes as well. "We do that when we're happy too."

Mom pulls her head back, her eyes wide, her mouth hanging open. "See!" she declares. "She's smart too!" Her head falls to my chest as she clings to the both of us, sobbing once again.

Nina's soft smile and the tear that falls down her cheek when her eyes meet mine make me want to pull her into my arms and kiss her hard, kiss her long, kiss her forever. But let's face it, with my mother in one arm and Nina in the other, it's a bit awkward – not to mention quite the boner killer – so I settle on kissing that tear away and placing another on her forehead.

I'll have her to myself when this day is over. I'll have her for the rest of my life because she said 'yes'. Nina is mine. She's really, really mine.

"This calls for a toast," dad says, filling a number of glasses with champagne and passing them out as each guest steps up to get one.

Every eye in the room is on us. Every smile belongs to us. They range from soft to amused to elated. Then I see Colt. In his smile I see happiness, acquiescence, and gratitude. Those lost years that we both suffered through. He longed for his Jannie and I longed for the girl no one knew about; the girl that believed I was redeemable. We didn't come through it all unscathed, but we both came out winners. He nods once, flashes a solemn wink and mouths, *"cradle robber."*

I mouth back, *"Asshole."* We exchange knowing grins and hold up our glasses in a private cheer.

"To winning," he says right before the glasses hit our lips.

You got that right, brother. In and out of the courtroom.

Epilogue

Five years and counting

"Here, baby, I got him," I tell my sweet wife as she lifts my future linebacker away from her stomach after feeling the wetness he's deposited upon waking from his nap. We're used to it. That little winky of his isn't so little and if you don't get it aimed in the right direction, he'll shoot right out the side and the diaper can't catch it before it leaks.

Oh, the struggles of being well hung.

We're all gathered for our monthly picnic with our best friends. This month it's being held at Colton and Jana's home, located on the edge of Lake Champlain – as are we all – separated only by a mile or two between us. Grayson and Kinzie are on the left while Nina and I are on the right. Unless of course your perspective is from the other side of the lake. Then Grayson and Kinzie are on the right and Nina and I are on the left. You get the picture. Unless you plan on arriving by boat or breaststroke, Nina and Sebastian are always right. And that's a foregone conclusion anyway, isn't it?

"S`ebastien," Nina warns, "I think he's about to…"

Too late. I've already got him against my shirt, my arm under his little snuggle butt, and now I am covered in . . .

The seventh grade and the football field.

Remember those old toilet paper commercials that told you "Don't squeeze the Charmin"? The same can be said for diapers. I'm sure there is an art for handling a child with a shitty diaper. I haven't learned it yet; probably never will. It doesn't matter.

"Somebody blasted their britches, didn't they?" I grin at my boy, not cuddling him any closer, but certainly not losing my grip on his tiny body as I turn toward the house where I will find the bathroom to clean him up and change his diaper and clothes – as well as my own from the feel of it. He's all of four weeks old and nursing like a champ, but the kid can shoot it out as fast as he sucks it down. Breast milk has advantages and disadvantages. The advantage being nutrients and building a strong immune system. The disadvantage being the need for a dozen wet wipes to change a shitty diaper and daddy's envy while my son lays claim to his mama's titties.

"Daddy!" my three and a half-year-old, Emily, calls as she runs on little legs next to her twin sister, Ainsley, to catch up. "Did Isaac poop on himself again?"

I chuckle, stopping to wait for both of them and Nina to catch up. "I think Isaac pooped on me this time too, Ems."

"Eww," she squeals, but then her mouth turns up in a precocious grin. "Are you gonna get the firehose?"

I've told them the football field story many times; the reason daddy doesn't like onesies. It's also the entire reason Grayson and Kinzie took great pleasure in gifting him with a dozen of them upon his arrival. All of them with cute little designs, one specially emblazoned with an iron-on picture of my face . . . on the ass.

I suppose I deserve a little bit of kickback. The T-shirt I got Gray for his last birthday probably wasn't well received by Kinzie – an arrow pointed toward his crotch with bold letters across the top: "Not lost; Wife Stole Them". It was that or "I'm With Stupid". I'll save that one for Kinzie.

"No firehose," Nina tells Ems, laughing. She opens the door to the house for me and leads the way into the bathroom just inside the entryway at the back next to the mudroom. She sets the enormous diaper bag on the counter and proceeds to lay the thick changing pad on top. "S`ebastien, I'll get you a change of clothes from the car."

I clear my throat loudly, scrunching my nose. "Nina, I'm thinking we might need a shower." The front of my shirt is smeared with a nice shade of baby-shit brown.

The back door opens and the outer room fills with women's chatter as Jana's, Nina's, and my mother enter. Nina's parents are here for the next month to enjoy another grandchild. If it makes my wife and kids happy, I'm happy.

"Grandma," Ainsley announces. "Isaac pooped on Daddy."

My mother peeks around the corner into the room where Isaac is already laid out on the counter on the changing pad, and I stand over him. I glance at my mom and smile as he starts to fuss.

"Want some help?" mom asks, taking in the mess on my shirt.

"Nah," I reply. "I'm good. If you could take the girls back outside, it would probably help. My man and I are going to shower this off."

Her face softens and her eyes water. "You're good at this, Sebastian. You remind me so much of your dad."

I smile at the sentiment. "Best compliment I could get, mom. Thanks."

Nina arrives with a fresh change of clothes for me, and mom takes the girls back outside – thankfully with the other mothers in tow as well. We've learned to pack extra clothes for ourselves when venturing out of the house for any length of time. With three kids, you never know what's going to get spilled, dropped, spit up, or in this case, shit out.

I strip out of my T-shirt and shorts while Nina undresses Isaac. Admittedly, she has the bigger chore. He fusses and tosses a fit once he stripped bare, but calms once he's in my arms. Nina starts the shower water – I trust her judgment for temperature more than my own. Once the water is tepid and ready for us to get in, I carefully step inside the shower, holding Isaac's little body like it's my lifeline.

Nina grabs the Baby Magic soap from the bag and stands at the door of the shower, pours some into her hand and gently caresses his little body with the wash, cleaning him head-to-toe, ensuring no remnants are left. She rubs a bit on my chest and the water carries the suds down toward my belly where it rinses and cleans me off as well. This isn't sensuous – it's intimate. And believe it or not, there is a difference.

Isaac only fusses a little. It's not like his normal baths where he screams so loudly and violently his little face turns red with a shade of purple mixed in. Once we're all rinsed, I step back from the flow of the water as Nina leans in to shut it off and turns to get a towel to wrap him in.

I study my son in my arms. He's just so beautiful; perfect really. His features are a reflection of Nina's eyes and dark hair, my chin, my nose and skin coloring. I lift him a little higher and kiss his forehead, feeling a sudden rush of warmth against my cheek. It's slight at first, then suddenly my ear begins to fill . . . with moisture.

"Nina," I say slowly, tilting my head to the side to drain the piss out of my ear as she reaches for Isaac, towel spread out in her hands. My slow, soft chuckle can't be contained as I lower him back to my chest and hold him close. "A little more water and a little more soap, please."

I love my life and I wouldn't change it for anything in the world.

The End

Other Books By This Author

The Crew Series:

Run To Me

Wicked Lemonade

Find Another Hero: Just Make Sure He Can Dance

Tell Me Why, Jannie

The Fresh French Connection

Old Farts and Pop Tarts

Saari, Not Sorry

The Chauffeur: Phoenix Rising

Manipulation 101: Code of Ethics

About the Author

A diehard laughaholic who has learned to take everything with a grain of salt, Annie Mick loves to dish it out with a good dose of sarcasm.

If you can giggle while you wiggle, it's added exercise and spares you ten minutes on the treadmill.

It is true that if you can laugh while you cry, the tears are saltier and it makes the margaritas taste better.

If you can find your hero in one of her books, therein lies her success. If you can find a bit of yourself in one her characters, therein lies her joy.

Life is too short to not get lost in a fantasy; if only for a day, if only in a book, one page at a time.

Sweet dreams.

www.ingramcontent.com/pod-product-compliance
Lightning Source LLC
Chambersburg PA
CBHW060319310726
48976CB00007B/2380